SWEET TEA

AND

SOUTHERN GRACE

GLENDA C. MANUS

Dedicated to my grandchildren:

to Chloe, who has inherited my love for the written word and has given me tips and encouragement during my writing journey;

to Genevieve, who also loves to write and whose loving nature and gentle heart gives me inspiration;

and to Jake, whose love of the Lord is calling him into the ministry.

Acknowledgments

A special thank you to my friends and family who have had to endure listening to me prattle and whine during my ups and downs of writing; to my daughters, Laura and Krista, who were my proofreaders and encouragers; to my husband, Henry, who was my biggest cheerleader; to my friends Terry and Genie Graham, who allowed me to photograph the front porch of their beautiful home for my cover; to the real Postmistress Betty, who allowed me to use her first name; and to the members of my Bible Study group who prayed specifically for this book to be pleasing to the Lord.

But most especially to the Lord, my God, for giving me the words to say.

"Every good and perfect gift is from above, coming down from the Father of lights, with whom there is no variation or shifting shadow." James 1:17

CHAPTER 1

Holly flexed her fingers and tried to relax her grip on the steering wheel. Her neck and shoulders were tense from hours of driving and the current weather conditions weren't helping. The last week had been an emotional one - she knew what she had to do - she didn't like it, but she had run out of options. Holly had come to this conclusion a few days earlier and she was now crossing the state-line into South Carolina on Interstate 77. The Charlotte lights were behind her and the bleakness of the night, along with her mood, engulfed her.

Five-year-old Abigail had kept her entertained for the first leg of the trip but was sound asleep by the time they crossed the border from Ohio into West Virginia. Holly glanced in the rearview mirror and saw she was still sleeping...her baby face snuggled against Bernie, her soft stuffed dog that she had slept with every night of her life.

"Please let her sleep – I don't need any distractions in this weather." She didn't know who she was appealing to - it seemed a remnant of a prayer to a God she was no longer sure she believed in. Streaks of lightning filled the sky and the booms of thunder that followed each strike were deafening. Rain was coming down in torrents now keeping the windshield wipers beating frantically.

Driving at night had never bothered Holly. In fact, it was normally a perfect time to travel with a little chatterbox who quickly became bored with riding long distances. Abby had been excited but puzzled as they drove away from their house. Simple explanations never worked with her and she asked question after question until Holly finally suggested that she cuddle up with Bernie and she would sing her favorite lullaby which promptly worked its magic. It was not your typical child's lullaby, this German love song. She began to sing it again as she drove – first in German and then in English. It was the song that Sonny sang to her when he first told her he loved her. His guitar in hand and down on one knee he began singing which had made her laugh. The smile in his eyes betrayed his mock indignation at being insulted with her laughter and he kept singing.

Du, du liegst mir im Herzen
du, du liegst mir im Sinn.
Du, du machst mir viel Schmerzen,
weißt nicht wie gut ich dir bin.
Ja, ja, ja, ja, weißt nicht wie gut ich dir bin.

He pulled her down on the floor beside him. "And why was that funny?"

"You should have seen yourself - you looked like something straight out of a Shakespearean play." She snuggled closer, "That was pretty - it's German, isn't it?"

"My mom used to sing it to us kids as a lullaby at night. I guess it just stuck with me. And yes, it's German. It's the tune from a music box my uncle brought back from Germany. Mom always said that singing it made her feel closer to her brother's spirit. He died right after he came home from the war."

"I like the tune. What do the words mean?"

"You would have to ask me," he said, trouching the tip of her nose. "It doesn't make much sense when you're translating from German to English, but I'll try. The star-crossed lover is saying that the girl he loves is always on his mind and in his heart, but she's indifferent about his feelings for her and it breaks his heart. The words are a declaration of how much she means to him and how much he cares for her."

"How sweet," she said. "A declaration of love."

"Yes," he said as he pulled her closer, "a declaration of love."

She now knew that his words were shallow, but at the time she had trusted him and believed everything he told her. He seemed so sincere and she had loved him. It was the end of his senior year at Ohio State University and as soon as he graduated, he took off to California for a dream job he had been offered in Silicon Valley, promising to keep in touch and to come back to see her as often as he could. She helped him load his Volkswagen with his few possessions and they clung to each other. "Call me so I'll know you got there safe and sound."

"Of course, I'll call," he had promised. She had been taking summer classes during the day and found a second shift job doing data entry for a bank operations center at night. She checked the answering machine when she got home each night and asked her father if Sonny had called. Each night it was the same answer - no calls. She searched the internet for his phone number, but he had not installed a land line. He had cancelled his cell phone service before he left since his employer had promised to provide him with one when he started work. Holly had never owned a cell phone – it was a luxury her parents couldn't afford after her mother's extended illness and the subsequent hospital bills.

As each day passed, she grew more concerned. She looked up his employer's phone number and called it. A receptionist answered. "Yes, he works here – would you like to speak with him?" She hung up the phone. He was safe – that's what she needed to know. He hadn't cared enough about her to call so she had no intentions of telling him what she had just learned - that he was going to be a father. Twenty, no husband and pregnant; it was an awful fix to be in, but she would go it alone. That had been six years ago and a lot had happened in those six years.

The dashboard clock read 3:36 a.m. They had been on the road nearly seven hours with only one stop. She was long past needing a bathroom break and in desperate need of a cup of coffee to keep her alert. She knew she should have stopped at the last truck stop and waited out the storm, but she was in such an all-fired hurry to get to the hotel. "Big mistake, Holly; big mistake," she said aloud while trying to see through the rain-soaked windshield. Park Place was less than twenty minutes away so she would wait. She had arranged for a hotel room just off the Interstate. She would catch a few hours of sleep and hope that Abby wouldn't wake up early. She turned up the volume of the radio and tried to find a station that would give weather updates. The way the car was swaying reminded her of the strong winds and tornados she had witnessed as a child in the Midwest before her family had moved to Ohio.

Holly had worried about her situation for the last month - ever since she got the news. How was Abby going to adjust to the days ahead? She wondered again if she had made the right decision - her mind felt as if it were in a fog - not capable of making decisions - but she had no family to turn to and no-one she trusted to advise her. Although this trip was no guaranteed solution, it was her only hope. Did his family even still live in the area? He had told her many stories of his childhood and she had envied him - envied his close-knit family and the small town that he seemed to love. Holly was an only child, her parents in their mid-forties when she was born - long after they had quit trying for a child. She'd had a good life, but with her mother's illnesses and her dad's withdrawal as a result, the last few years had been lonely.

Park Place, South Carolina - population eight thousand - she had looked it up on a map and almost needed magnifying glasses to find it. Over the last few weeks, she had made efforts again to contact Sonny in California but his home number was private and he had changed employers. Then she thought about his family in the South and finally made up her mind to just show up on their doorstep. If she called ahead, they may reject her just as Sonny had done. Would they accept what she would tell them? I hope so, she thought; for Abby's sake, I really hope so.

The windshield wipers were still going strong, but the rain was too much for them - she could barely see the tail lights of the cars ahead of her. The storm seemed to be following her, but what the heck - her life had just been one storm after another anyway. She pushed a wayward strand of hair behind her ear. As a jagged streak of lightning lit the sky, it illuminated her pale skin and auburn hair. The wind was blowing harder. "Hang on Abby," she said aloud even though Abby was still sleeping. "I've got to pull over – this isn't safe." Other cars were pulling off the road and Holly followed the car ahead as it slowly made its way onto the shoulder. Now maybe she could relax.

She felt the ground shake and heard a cracking sound before she saw what was happening. She looked up through the windshield just in time to see a huge limb from the tree on the bank of the road as it made its way down toward the car. Her only thoughts were of Abby. "Oh God" she cried out, "Please watch over my baby." She heard a scream and realized it was her own as she slipped into unconsciousness.

CHAPTER 2

"*I urge, then, first of all, that requests, prayers, intercession and thanksgiving be made for everyone,*"

~ 1 Timothy 2: 1, 2

As the sounds of sirens filled the air, Rock turned over and looked at the clock on the bedside table - 3:50 a.m. The first siren had not quite penetrated his deep sleep, but had woven itself into his dream. He had been riding fast and carefree on a motorcycle down a winding country road. The next siren brought him closer to wakefulness though he tried hard to will himself back to sleep to finish the dream and find out where he was going. The third and final siren brought him fully awake and to the realization that something bad was happening in the idyllic little town of Park Place. This is a knee bender he thought, as he quickly pulled the sheets back and got out of bed. The rain and thunderstorms during the night had cooled the air considerably and the room was chilly for mid-May. The lightning strikes lit up the room enough for him to find his robe without having to turn on the lamp. He slipped it on and immediately knelt at the side of the four-poster bed. He wondered what it was; a house fire caused by lightning? Or maybe an accident on the interstate. Whatever it was, it must be serious with all those sirens.

"Lord God," he said aloud. "This is in your hands. Be

compassionate and merciful to those who are hurt and guide the hands of the ones who are caring for them. God, I cry out to you on their behalf. Heal their wounds and wrap your loving arms around them so they will not be fearful. I ask these things in the name of your Son, Jesus Christ. Amen."

He stayed on his knees talking to God and then a while longer just listening. When he finished he got up and turned on the bedside lamp - there was no use in trying to go back to sleep. His wild motorcycle dream was over and he wondered what part of his sub-conscious mind it had come from. As a teenager growing up in rural Georgia, he had wanted a motorcycle – "just a small one to go back and forth to school," he had pleaded with his parents. He could see his father bending a little but his overprotective mother had won out in the end. Maybe a remnant of that longing from years ago, he thought as he made his way into the kitchen to make a pot of coffee. Theo heard him stirring around and jumped off the clothes dryer in the utility room where he slept. He dragged into the kitchen stretching both front feet before him and looked up at Rock as if wondering what he was doing up in the middle of the night. Theo reached his paws up for Rock to rub him behind the ears. After a few seconds of a gentle ear massage, Theo turned around and bit him making Rock jerk his hand back and wonder why he had rescued the cantankerous, moody cat.

Rock had never owned a cat until the scraggly kitten had appeared on his back porch. It was a day of torrential rains and as Rock checked the locks on the back door before going to bed, he heard a faint, pitiful little sound coming from the direction of the outdoor grill. He found Theo - wet, shivering and half-starved under the meager shelter of the grill. He brought him inside, gave him a warm bath and dried him off with a hand towel. He then chopped up a piece of deli ham in a bowl of warm milk and watched as the kitten gobbled it up. He laughed as Theo growled at him when he tried to move the bowl.

Not knowing what to do with a cat, he had called his friend Liz who told him to shred up some newspapers and put them in one corner of a box and a towel in the other corner. The newspapers would serve as a litter box until he could go out the next morning and buy one.

"I don't want him getting too cozy. I'm giving him away."

"Right," she had said, "Good luck!" Her tone implyed that she knew something he didn't and then she hung up. He wondered what she meant by that. From her groggy voice, he knew he had called too late, but she hung up so fast he didn't get a chance to apologize.

Much to his dismay, the next morning he found that the kitten had pooped all over the towel and slept on the shredded newspapers. This was an omen of things to come. The kitten was so emaciated and pitiful looking, he had no luck in giving him away.

"It's hard to find homes for cute kittens, much less ugly ones," one of his church members had said. And the cat would continue to be cantankerous but he had learned to love the quirky little fellow and his eccentric nature even though he knew he must be staying up nights planning ways to terrorize the house.

"That's normal," Liz told him. "Cats are independent

little creatures and they don't play by anyone's rules."

"How do you know so much about cats?"

"I've had one before."

"Well, take this one. Please."

"Finders keepers; losers weepers."

"I won't weep, I promise you." But no amount of pleading worked with Liz.

The upside was that Theo took to the litter box as if he had been born to it. There was never another accident but after the big visit to the vet to be neutered, he became mad and sulky and started attacking Rock's feet every time he would walk around a corner. When he was hungry, he would scamper through the house knocking things off tables and dressers until Rock got up and fed him. But even with all his craziness, each time Rock sat down to study for his sermons or to read a book, Theo would curl up beside him – sometimes on his lap, but most of the time in the crook of his arm and go fast asleep, content with his little world.

He took his cup of coffee into his study and turned on the floor lamp beside the big leather armchair. The thunderstorm had moved on and the heavy rain was beginning to ease a little. His Bible was on the arm of the chair where he had left it the night before. He pulled it into his lap out of habit. Theo followed and jumped into his lap hoping for some attention. Rock's thoughts drifted back to his family – his mom and dad who still lived in Georgia near his two sisters and their families. They came to visit him often but they never stayed long. They were always in a hurry to get back to the grandchildren. When he teased his mother about it, she had answered back a little too smugly in her genteel Southern accent. "Well, I do declare, Rockford Williford Clark. If I didn't know better, I'd think you were jealous. If you would just get married and have some kids of your own, I would visit you more often." Their visits seemed to always end on that note.

Rock had never liked his name - it sounded stuffy. He could understand Rockford - it was his mother's maiden name - but Williford, for heaven sakes. Where did that come from? His mother was evasive and always acted insulted that he didn't like what she had named him. His dad had once confided that he had tried his best to change her mind about the name when he was born, but she wouldn't budge. At least they had shortened it to Rock. His father had insisted over his mother's objections. "Irene, be reasonable," his father had told her. "The boy will be tormented with a name like that. I'm not going to have a son of mine being bullied because of his name." He had given her a choice of Rock or Will and she gave in. "Ah, Rock; now that does sound rather masculine, doesn't it? I'm so glad I thought of it."

"Typical Irene," his father had told him, "always taking credit for my ideas, but I wasn't a bit surprised - she always was a little enamored with Rock Hudson."

Rock was never bullied but over the years he had taken some ribbing about his name. When the old hymn, Rock of Ages was played in church, his sisters would snicker and point to him. When he learned to play the guitar in high school, his friends called him Rock 'n Roll. But the name that had stuck like glue was the one he now lived with – Rev Rock. Upon graduation from seminary, his first congregation had struggled with what to call him. The Methodist minister in the neighborhood was called Preacher Tom. The Baptist minister was Pastor Rick. The Catholic priest was Father Nathaniel and the Reformed Presbyterian minister was Reverend Clark. Rock was only twenty-five when he came to Park Place Presbyterian with an active church membership of one hundred and four. The Session members had discussed that it was unfortunate that both Presbyterian ministers in town had the same last name - two Reverend Clarks would be confusing. They toyed with calling him simply by his first name, but found it to be too casual. They settled on Reverend Rock and over the years shortened it to Rev Rock. Most everyone in town still called him that except for a few close friends.

***

Theo broke the silence with his shrill meowing. Rock got up from the armchair. "Ok, old boy, time for your cheerios." He walked back into the kitchen and picked up the bag of cat food. He shook the bag and Theo rounded the corner in a flash. The kitchen was dark except for the light over the sink which he always kept on. He flipped the switch on the wall and the large industrial style kitchen shone brilliantly in all its stainless-steel glory and once again he wished that the designer the Session had insisted on hiring to decorate the house had gone for a warmer, cozier look. He flipped the lights back off and put two pieces of wheat bread in the toaster. "I prefer to eat in the dark, don't you Theo?" At the same moment the bread popped up, the phone rang. The phone was beside the toaster and with a start Rock picked up a slice of toast and put it to his ear and said, "Hello."

CHAPTER 3

*G*od is our refuge and strength, an ever-present help in trouble. Therefore, we will not fear, though the earth give way and the mountains fall into the heart of the sea.

~ Psalms 46: 1-2 NIV

From the road, all you could see was a splash of white at the end of the driveway, but as Rock drew closer to the house, the full splendor of the massive columns, the wide porch veranda, and the flower laden rose trellises once again took his breath away. Amidst a grove of pecan trees at the end of a pencil thin driveway, Beverly Hills stood in all its majestic glory. Rock marveled at the manicured lawn, the well-shaped shrubbery, the abundance of tulips and daylilies, and realized that this was no small feat for the single caretaker, Jeb Hawkins, to achieve this look.

Beverly Hills Children's Home was a converted antebellum house once owned by Dr. John Beverly, a decorated WWII veteran who had willed it to the Church with explicit instructions that it be only used to house children in need of assistance. The church had complied by leasing it out to a philanthropic organization that worked with the state agencies in finding homes for children. Beverly Hills was often referred to as "the orphanage," but it was much more than that. It was true that some of the residents were orphaned by one or both parents, but the majority had been taken away from drug addicted or abusive parents. They were placed at Beverly Hills as "long-termers" – the ones deemed with little or no hope of being placed back with their parents.

The truck's tires crunched as he made his way under the tight canopy of pecan trees. The pecans from these trees had found their way into many a pecan pie over the years. Although every woman in Park Place had her own favorite recipe, they all admitted that Estelle Walker made the best pecan pie east of the Mississippi River. Estelle had once confided that the secret to her pies was the smidgen of corn meal she used to bind it. There must be something else, Rock thought, because when she let that little secret out, there had been a run on corn meal at Lloyd Mills' Grocery Store but no one ever accomplished Estelle's perfection. She had been Beverly Hill's cook for as long as Rock could remember.

He had recovered from his toast mishap in time to catch Rebecca's phone call. "Rock, can you come out for a visit? We have a new addition."

"Sure, just give me time to eat my toast. I have Mabel Tarlton's blackberry jelly here on the counter ready to spread it on."

Rebecca laughed, "It would be cruel if I insisted you come out before you eat Mabel's jelly. I can't resist it either."

"This one will break your heart," she said before she hung up. They always break my heart, thought Rock as he stepped out of his truck onto the brick paved courtyard. Brick, brick, brick – everything in Park Place was paved with old, hand molded brick that came from the early years of the local brick factory. Ed Simmons, the sales manager at the brick factory had once said that if every brick in Park Place was placed in single file, they would stretch all the way to California.

He started up the walkway which led to a grand stairway sweeping up to the veranda. White rockers lined the side of the wrap-around porch that faced the rose garden. An angelic figural fountain was in the midst of the garden, spilling water into the Koi pond below. He reached the doorway where two tall benches flanked either side. The door was open and Rock knocked on the screen. When no one answered, he stepped into the foyer and peeked inside. The room to the left had once been a grand ballroom but had now been converted into two rooms – half of it a large recreational room with several seating areas, a ping-pong table, video games and a TV. Double French doors led to the other half which was now a dining hall.

This Thursday morning was not much different than any other weekday morning. The older children were at school. Three-year-old Carson was banging loudly on a keyboard in one corner of the room while the TV played softly in another corner. One of the four-year-old twins. Ava or Emma, he couldn't tell them apart, was putting together a Dora the Explorer puzzle on the floor. Rock bent over to help. "Here you go, put the outside pieces together first and then the others just fall into place." At the sound of his voice, a scurry of little feet came running to greet him. This was the fun part. Rebecca faithfully drove her school bus loaded with caregivers and kids of all ages to church every Sunday morning. Along with staff members, she dropped some off at the Baptist Church, some at the Methodist and the rest she brought to her own church, Park Place Presbyterian. These were the children Rock knew by name. At one time or another each of the older ones had been an acolyte and each one had been the subject of his humble prayers to the Lord.

Rebecca got up from the rocking chair in the corner and put her knitting on the small footstool in front of it. "It looks like they're all glad to see you. I told them you were coming." She walked over and gave Rock a hug which started a cascade of hugs from the other children in the room. After the hugs were over and the children went back to their games, Rock pulled up a chair beside Rebecca's. Rebecca picked up her knitting and sat back down. "Rock, I suppose you heard about the accident last night out on the highway during the storm."

"So that's what happened? Judging by the number of sirens, I thought it must be a fire or a bad accident. I couldn't go back to sleep." He waited for Rebecca to go on.

"It was bad Rock. There was a young woman and a little girl in the car - apparently her daughter. The woman's injuries were serious, but the little girl didn't have a scratch. You know how that stretch of the road is lined with trees – some with limbs hanging over the road? Well, lightning struck a tree and a large limb fell right on the front of the car crashing through the windshield. The car caught on fire, but the rain doused it before it spread."

"Thank God for that." said Rock. "What's their condition this morning?"

"That's what I wanted to talk to you about. I haven't

heard anything more about the condition of the mother, but Jess brought the little girl back here after she had been checked out at the hospital. They didn't get here until 4:30 or so this morning. Poor little thing, she was all tuckered out and is still sleeping. I felt bad for Jess too - he had to go back to the police station this morning after getting almost no sleep." She paused.

"I hope he doesn't get in trouble for not calling social services first. He said the child was just so distraught, it would have been cruel to make her wait for someone to get to the hospital and question her. He figured they would bring her here anyway – they always do."

Rock smiled, "Well at least he's the chief. He can't get into too much trouble. How old is the child?"

"I really don't know. She looks to be about four or five. It's funny - I don't know her name yet. She was sound asleep when Jess brought her in - didn't even wake up when I changed her into pajamas and put her in bed. I was hoping you would get here before I woke her up. She's sharing a room with the twins. I'm going to go check on her - you want to come with me?"

Beverly Hills was a large sprawling three-story house. The main three stories were used as living space. The attic was used for storing odd furniture, suitcases and extra clothing for the children. A set of stairs in the kitchen led down to the cellar where the food and kitchen equipment was stored.

The first floor was still magnificent even after all the changes that had been made, out of necessity, for turning it into a home for children. The foyer in the center of the house still had a very formal look with original artwork and paneled wainscoting still intact. To the right of the foyer was another sitting area for visitors. A large library with conference tables was beyond the sitting area and was used for board meetings and family counseling. Beyond the library was a master suite with a bedroom, bath and a small living room. This was where Rebecca and her husband Jess lived.

There was a large hallway past the foyer which led into the large commercial kitchen on the right and the converted dining hall on the left. The architect responsible for the conversion had used every bit of available space effectively.

There were five bedrooms on the second floor which currently housed twelve girls. Each room had two bunk beds and could sleep four children, except for the smaller bedroom to the left of the staircase which was the female counselor's room.

The blueprint of the third floor was an exact replica of the second and it housed the boys and the male counselor.

Rebecca and Rock stopped on the second floor. Penny Wilson was the girls' counselor and was just coming out of her room. She motioned to Rebecca. "I just heard her stirring around and was going in to take a look."

"Thanks Penny, we'll take it from here," Rebecca said as she turned to the left with Rock following behind her. Rock froze in place as he heard a child's scream coming from the door at the end of the hallway.

***

Shush, baby, shush." Rebecca was sitting on the bed holding the child in her arms swaying back and forth when Rock walked into the room.

"Mommy! Where's my Mommy?" Rebecca's soothing voice was beginning to have a calming effect on the little girl and her sobs were fading away.

"Rock, maybe this wasn't such a good idea. Why don't I get her calmed down and dressed and we'll meet you downstairs for breakfast?" Rock didn't hesitate and got out of there as fast as he could. Tears always did him in.

He was sitting at the counter with Estelle when Rebecca walked into the kitchen holding the little girl's hand. "Estelle, meet Abigail," she said. "I think she's hungry!"

"Abigail, is it? I kept breakfast warm just for you Miss Abigail, but I was beginning to think you were going to sleep the day away. I saved you one of Estelle's famous butter biscuits. I'll dribble some honey on top and fix you right up." Rebecca lifted her up on the barstool beside Rock and Estelle put the plate in front of her. "You do like honey, don't you baby?"

Abigail smiled. "Yes ma'am, I do," she said.

"Well I'll be!" exclaimed Estelle. "This child has got some manners." Abigail sat quietly with her hands in her lap and looked at Rebecca for affirmation. Rebecca winked at her.

"It's fine Sweetie, you can go ahead and eat." Abigail looked around.

"Who's turn to say the blessing?" she asked. The three

adults looked at one another.

"Why I think it's my turn," Rock said.

"And I think we've all been put in our place," said Rebecca. They all laughed and joined hands as Rock thanked God for each and every one of the people in this household and to bless the honey biscuit Abigail was about to eat.

Rock watched as Abigail wolfed down the biscuit and asked for another. Estelle beamed as she put another biscuit on the plate.

"It's alright, isn't it Miss Rebecca?"

"Sure Estelle, we'll worry about a balanced diet later. I'm glad to see such an appetite!" As she finished eating, Abigail turned to Rock.

"Are you the preacher?" Rock smiled and nodded his head. He was surprised at how well-mannered and articulate the child was.

"Miss Rebecca said you would pray for my Mommy. She's in the hospital and I'll get to play with the children here until she gets better."

"Abigail, I'm honored that you asked me to pray for her. I'll go by to see her today and let you know later how she's getting along." The little girl smiled and reached over to hug him.

"Thank you, preacher and you may call me Abby." As he held the little girl in his arms, his heart went out to her.

"And you can call me Rev Rock. All the other children do." She was in a strange place with strange people and she seemed to be taking it all in stride. He knew it had a lot to do with Rebecca's way of working with children, but it was also apparent that she'd had a good upbringing.

"May I be excused?" she asked. Without waiting for an answer, she slipped off the stool and scampered down the hallway.

"She's making herself right at home," Rebecca said smiling. Rock looked over at her and shook his head in disbelief.

"You make it look so easy."

Rebecca walked with Rock to the door. As they passed the playroom, they peeked inside and saw Abigail on the floor in front of the puzzle.

"I see Emma's letting her help put it together," Rebecca said.

Rock smiled, "So Emma it is? I can never tell them apart."

As he opened the door to walk out on the porch, he heard Emma say, "If you put the outside pieces together Abby, it'll just fall in place."

***

Rock went by the police station after he left Beverly Hills. Jess Hamilton wasn't in but Officer Cliff Jordan had been assigned to find the young woman's family back in Columbus to inform them of the accident.

"Rock, we've not had much luck locating her family. Holly Spencer is the name on the driver's license and her address is listed as Columbus, Ohio. The license plate on her car verifies that. As I said, we haven't found any relatives yet but we asked the Columbus Police

Department to talk with her neighbors. They've done that and they've also found where she worked. I've already talked to her employer."

When Rock left, he had all the information Cliff had gathered. He sat in the car for a minute and wondered how he had managed to get himself involved. It seemed he was always a magnet for other people's troubles. I'll just visit the mother and be on my way, he thought. How difficult could it be?

CHAPTER 4

From an outside view, Clancy Memorial Hospital looked more imposing than it really was. The new addition sat very close to the street which made it look higher than its five floors. Rock pulled into the parking lot and thought of the conversation he had just had with Officer Jordan about the accident. No family - it was puzzling, but surely they would locate someone. As he parked in one of the parking spaces reserved for Clergy, he saw Lonnie Welch sitting in the EMS van writing up his latest case reports. He walked up and tapped on the passenger side window and a startled Lon jumped and papers went flying everywhere. Lon reached over and rolled down the window with a sheepish grin on his face. "If you weren't a preacher, I'd be a cussin' – you 'bout near scared me to death."

Rock laughed, "Let me help you pick up your papers."

"Nah... Believe it or not, I have a system going here. They're not too scattered. You got something on your mind – hop in and sit a spell." He cleared off the passenger seat and Rock got in.

"Lon, can you give me any information on the young woman in the accident Monday night?" Lonnie put his papers down.

"I don't even know her name, Rev Rock. I saw she had an out of state license plate but I was so busy working with her that I didn't have time to ask any questions. Who is she - and how about the little girl? I heard she's over at the orphanage."

Rock relayed some of the information to Lon. "Holly Spencer is the mother - she's from Columbus, Ohio, but right now she's somewhat of a mystery. The Columbus police are trying to get some answers. The little girl's name is Abby and she's all settled in with Rebecca at Beverly Hills. As a matter of fact, she's got them all bedazzled - especially Estelle." Lon looked up from his paperwork.

"They should send me up there to Columbus, Ohio. My wife says I can find out more in ten minutes than she can in ten days."

Rock didn't doubt it. "I've heard it told that you can talk the hair off a Billy goat's ear."

Lon grinned. "You must'a been talking to my wife."

Rock smiled. "I'm not telling." He watched as the young man continued picking up papers and putting them in folders.

"Lon, I was wondering if Miss Spencer was responsive at all when you pulled her out of the car?"

He started to shake his head, but stopped and looked up. "Well, come to think of it, she was - just for a few seconds. As I was cutting her seatbelt, she kept muttering a word over and over. She kept saying the word 'sunny' over and over. I told her, '*Ma'am, I wish it was sunny. It would be a whole lot easier getting you out of this car if it wasn't pouring down rain.* That was the last thing I heard her say. After that her vitals pretty much plummeted until we got her in the van and stabilized. But she never said another word after that. I don't know why she was so interested in the weather at a time like that."

"Thanks Lon, I'll go in and see if there's any change in her condition this morning. I'm going to by the coffee shop first – join me for a cup?"

"Had mine a couple of hours ago Rev Rock, but before ya' go in, let me tell you a little joke since you were ribbing me about talking so much. It makes me think a' my wife."

"I can always use a good laugh."

"Well now, here it is. Everybody on earth dies and goes to heaven. God comes and says, "I want the men to form two lines -- one for the men that dominated their women on earth, and the other line for the men who were dominated by their women. Also, I want all the women to go with St. Peter." The next time God looks, the women are all gone, and there are two lines. The line for the men who were dominated by their women was 100 miles long, but in the line of men who were the dominators, there was only one man. God got mad and his voice boomed, "You men should be ashamed of yourselves. I created you in my image, and you were all whipped by your mates. Look at the only one of my sons who stood up and made me proud. Learn from him! Tell them, boy, how did you manage to be the only one in this line?" The man turned around and looked at all the other men and trembled. "I don't know," he said, "my wife told me to stand over here."

Rock was still laughing when he climbed out of the van and walked toward the hospital entrance. He looked back to wave but Lon was bent over the seat cleaning up the scattered papers.

As he waited for the elevator, he saw several familiar

faces. Life goes on, he thought, even though we're sidelined with illnesses, afflictions and obstacles to overcome, it's just for a moment. Children are still laughing and playing, the birds are still singing and night turns into day. There is much more to life than temporary things - thank God for that. The elevator door opened and he stepped in.

***

Rock walked up to the nurse's station and was relieved to see Jamie Webster was on duty. Bessie and Sammy Webster had put all their children through college. Bessie owned a small house cleaning service and Sammy and his brother had a successful concrete business. Jamie had been a bonus baby - born several years after they thought they were done having children. Even though it meant "working forevermore" as Bessie had put it, they gave her the same opportunity as the other children and she went to school to get her nursing degree. She was the highlight of Rock's trips to the hospital when he had a patient on her floor. She loved her job and the patients loved her. Her smile was contagious and she flashed one at Rock now. "Well, if it's not my favorite preacher!" She did a little dance that made Rock laugh.

Her smile faded when he started asking questions about the patient. "Dr. Braem hasn't been in yet this morning, but Holly had a restless night. It's time for me to go off duty in about twenty minutes, but I'm hanging around until he comes in."

"Has she come out of the coma yet?"

"The coma was induced and she's still heavily medicated. I'll let Dr. Braem tell you more when he gets here." Rock knew it was no use to push it. Jamie took her job seriously and a patient's privacy was to be honored unless there was written consent. Rock wondered how much Pete Braem could tell him.

"I've got to run up one floor and see Danny McCarthy. He was admitted yesterday for a respiratory infection. If Pete comes in before I get back, ask him to have me paged."

"I'll do that Rev Rock. Oh, did I tell you how handsome and dapper you look this morning – maybe you've got a new girlfriend or something?" Rock laughed as he walked down the hall.

"Don't hold your breath Jamie. I don't see anyone beating on my door to find me."

"You need to be the one beating on doors. We women like to be courted, not the other way around!" She smiled and started whistling as she made her way to room number 114 where Mrs. Yancey was waiting on her bath.

When Rock returned to the first floor, an intern pointed in the direction of the doctor's office. "Last door on the right - his name is on the door." The door was closed and the small plaque read: *Dr. Peter Braem, Neurologist.*

Rock knocked and heard a voice telling him to come in. Dr. Braem's office in the hospital was sparse. He sat behind a small desk with only a laptop, a prescription pad, and a stack of patient folders in front of him. A small bookcase behind his desk held a few medical books that were flanked on each side by a pair of sailboat bookends. An enlarged photo of a sailboat was hanging on the wall behind the bookcase. Rock wondered if sailing was a pastime for the doctor. Dr. Braem had been at Clancy Memorial for a little over a year and had earned a reputation as a quiet but competent doctor, but Rock had never heard much about his social life. He had bumped into him in the cafeteria once and they sat and had lunch together. Since then they had become casual friends, but neither had much more time than to acknowledge the other in the hospital corridors.

"Anything you can tell me, Pete? Rebecca called me this morning to come out to Beverly Hills and meet Abby, Holly Spencer's daughter. She's asked me to provide pastoral care and act as a liaison if I can between the child and her mother while she's in the hospital. Abby is anxious and I would like to reassure her. Of course, I don't want to get her hopes up if the prognosis is poor."

Dr. Braem smiled. "I wondered how you got involved. You preachers are pulled in many directions, aren't you?"

"Like we're in a tug of war game, I'm afraid, and it never ends until the rope gets frayed in the middle and we fall over."

"It happens to doctors too, but most of the time it's more like Pin the Tail on the Donkey with us. I sometimes feel like I have blinders on trying to search out the answers. But in answer to what you can tell the little girl, I think it's safe to tell her that her mom is sleeping a lot and can't have visitors for a while but as soon as she can, we'll get her in here to see her. Children seem to think in simple terms. I think that'll satisfy her. She's about the age of my oldest daughter so she'll have some questions, but at that age, they pretty much trust what you tell them. Do the police know yet if she has any family?"

"Cliff Jordan is working on it - he doesn't have a clue yet on what Holly is doing in Park Place. From what Cliff has been able to determine, she had a good job as a computer analyst for a bank in Columbus. She walked into her supervisor's office a few days ago and gave notice that she would be cleaning out her office and leaving immediately. She gave no reason why. Her supervisor told him that Holly had been on medical leave for a couple of months last year, but had mentioned no recent problems. He was pretty upset that she left them in a bind with no thought of a replacement. So far the police haven't been able to locate any next of kin."

"Rock, as you know, the HIPAA act limits the information we can give on our patients to anyone other than immediate family. The only way I could go into details about her condition is if someone would become her guardian in charge of making her medical decisions while she's in no condition to make them herself. I've never had a case like this; we've always been able to locate family, but she had no emergency numbers in her wallet.

"Thanks Pete, I understand the rules. I'll see what I can do and come back tomorrow if you have time to see me."

"Sure thing - I should finish my rounds around 10:30."

CHAPTER 5

*L*ove is patient and kind; love does not envy or boast; it is not arrogant or rude. It does not insist on its own way; it is not irritable or resentful; it does not rejoice at wrongdoing, but rejoices with the truth. Love bears all things, believes all things, hopes all things, endures all things.

~ Corinthians 13:4-7 ESV

Rock's office was big and spacious and was located between the church and the new manse. It had once been a carriage house that sat behind a larger main house owned by the Stillmans, whose ancestors were some of the founding members of Park Place Presbyterian. They were a wealthy family owning many large parcels of land in the community. The carriage house had been part stable, part garage in the days of horse and carriages. When Ned Stillman died a few years after his wife, the Officers of the church were called to the reading of the will and were delighted to learn that he had left the house and property to the church.

They had rented the Stillman House out for a while until the maintenance on it had become burdensome and was not generating enough revenue to make it worthwhile to rent. The Maintenance & Grounds Committee suggested tearing the house down. The church was growing and with growth came the need of new Sunday School classrooms. It had always been in the back of their minds to build a new manse since the old manse was a small cottage style house built in the 1920's located further back on the property. Their reasoning was that their minister was still young enough to marry and have children and would eventually need a bigger home. There were several wealthy members of the church who were generous with their giving, so money was no object and the sale of the old manse could help defer the cost.

The carriage house was remodeled, the old offices became Sunday School rooms and the new manse became a reality. As soon as Rock had moved into the new house, the little cottage that had been the manse was sold for quite a good sum. The new house was nice but noisier because of its close proximity to the busy street traffic. The old manse sat nestled in a small grove of oaks at the end of the little winding driveway that ran behind the new office. It was tucked away from view at the very back of the church property almost backing up to the little used side street behind it. Truth be known, he had been quite fond of the little cottage and its wrap-around porch and had been very despondent about moving out.

He was surprised to see his reserved parking space was empty. Reva almost always parked in it, but today her car was in one of the spaces reserved for visitors. As he parked, she rushed out the door to greet him with a big smile on her face and her warm chocolate complexion glowing with excitement. She waved at him with both hands while trying to talk coherently. "Rev Rock, Rev Rock, I tried to reach you at the hospital. They paged you but you never answered. Carly Higgins had her baby boy this morning and he weighed in at 9 pounds, 4 ounces. I don't know how that tiny little woman had that big baby boy."

Rock watched with amusement until she stopped. "Reva - why didn't you just call me on my cell phone?" Reva smacked her forehead. "I didn't think about the cell phone. But anyway, it's not normal to have some tiny little gadget not big enough to spit at to call somebody on," Reva complained. "Besides, you sound like you're in a tin can when I talk to you."

"Well, if I had known about the baby, I would have stopped by to see Carly before I left - now I'll have to make another trip to the hospital." He sighed.

Reva put her hands on her hips. "Now don't you go fussin' at me Reverend Clark."

Uh oh, he thought. When Reva used his formal title, he knew he was in for it. "That Carly don't want a preacher getting in her business right after having a baby, don't you know? Having a baby is hard work - she'll be wantin' some quiet time and some time to be lovin' on that baby boy!"

"I'm sorry Reva - I wasn't fussing, honestly.... but I guess I did sound like an old bear." He had some backtracking to do and he prattled on. "I don't think I've ever seen anyone get so excited about babies. It seems like after six of your own and a passel of grandkids you'd be tired of babies by now."

The mention of babies wiped the frown off her face. "I'll never get tired of babies. I just love how they feel in your arms...those sweet little bodies so helpless and all. They just nuzzle right up to you and it makes my heart go all fuzzy inside, yes it does. And their sweet smell of baby powder and burps! Why if they could make a fragrance that smelled like that, they couldn't keep it on the shelves."

Rock looked skeptical. "I've experienced quite a few spit-ups during my years of baptizing babies, and I can tell you right now Reva; I wouldn't give you two cents for the scent of baby burp." Reva laughed.

"Ah, you say that now, but if you were to ever have a little 'un of your own, you would be talking a different story. And by the way, you should'a done married and had you a baby by now. Why you must be going nigh on forty-five and haven't even found yourself a wife. That's a shame, yes it is!" Rock just shook his head and laughed. They'll never give up, he thought and walked into his office, turned the coffee maker on and shut the door.

***

For a few years after coming to Park Place, Rock had felt under pressure. Everyone in the church wanted him married and each one knew the perfect woman for him. He had gone out a few times, but nothing ever came of it. Last year he had gone out with a real estate agent from nearby Chester a few times, but after he learned she had been married three times already and was only 36, he quickly backed out of the relationship. He just wasn't meant to marry; if so, God would have brought someone into his life. But that wasn't quite true, he thought. God had brought someone. His mind drifted back to his college years.

Rock had found himself mesmerized by the young

woman's eyes. "Violet" he said out loud. The girl sitting opposite him in the musty school library gave him a puzzled glance. "Your eyes – they're not blue, they're not grey – they're violet," he said with satisfaction. She gave him a smile that knocked his socks off. Against everyone's objections, three months later they announced their engagement. Jan's parents objected because she was too young. She was twenty-one and just a junior on the same college campus where Rock was in Seminary. Rock was 24 and in his last year of Louisville Theological Seminary working toward his Master of Divinity degree. But he had known from the moment of that smile there could never be anyone else to fill him with the kind of ethereal wonder other than God himself.

"Why wait," he said. "Neither of us wants a big wedding and life is too short not to spend it together." He had thought about this statement many times over the years and was grateful that they had made a commitment to each other. He would have never known the blissful contentment of being engaged to the girl with the violet eyes if they had waited.

It was swift and silent. The semester had been hectic and they were enjoying a rare Saturday morning cup of coffee at the campus coffee shop. As they were catching up, Jan's hand started shaking and she dropped her coffee cup. Rock jumped up to make sure she hadn't burned herself and the waitress ran over to clean it up.

"Too much caffeine," she said as she took the extra napkin from the waitress and dabbed at the coffee on her jeans.

"Are you sure you're okay?"

"Sure, I'm just a little stressed."

Why had he not noticed the subtle little things – the occasional memory losses that they both attributed to busy schedules - laughing that when they both got their churches, he would have to remind her where she put her sermons; the dark circles under her eyes that they thought were caused by long study hours. But during the hours they carved out for each other, they clung to the dream of spending their life together and raising a family. When exams were over and they were celebrating one night with a glass of wine, Jan's right hand started the same trembling as with the coffee cup, but this time her whole body began shaking. The ambulance ride seemed never ending as Jan endured repeated seizures and Rock prayed like he had never prayed before. Even before they ran the first round of tests, the doctor suspected a brain tumor. The tests, scans and ultrasounds revealed that the small, insignificant looking mole she had put off having checked was melanoma and it had spread throughout her body.

Rock had prayed, oh how he had prayed. He remembered one night at the end of a heartfelt on-your-knees prayer – "Oh God, if you can't make her better, take me with her. I don't want to live without her." But he had. Yes, it had been swift and silent – one month after they had celebrated with the glass of wine, the light in the violet eyes dimmed forever and a little bit of him dimmed with them.

The aroma of coffee brought him out of his reverie. "Enough," he said, as he raised his cold coffee cup to his lips and then sat it back down. "Now God, allow me talk to you about Holly Spencer," and on his knees once more, he poured out his heart, giving it all to the One who could handle it best.

He looked at the small adamantine clock on his desk as it gave two loud chimes. The clock had always set on the mantle in his grandparent's home when he was a child, and was one of the few items he had wanted when his Nana passed away. Two p.m. and he hadn't had lunch. He opened his office door and looked at Reva sheepishly. She had been working on the new church directory, but looked up when she heard the door open. "Why you lookin' like a little hound dog puppy?" she said.

"Well, I was hoping there might be something for me to raid out of the refrigerator."

"Honey, you know I've always got something in the fridge – you just help yourself. There's a big ole' ham biscuit that I brought leftover from breakfast this morning and there's some chicken and dumplings I made just for you – thought you might like to have 'em for your dinner tonight but they eat just as easy for lunch."

"Dinner it is! I'll just eat the biscuit for now. You're trying to pack some pounds on me Reva - but I'm not complaining. You're the best cook in the county." He warmed the biscuit in the microwave and went back to his office.

He was still nibbling the biscuit as he picked up the phone. "Bob, I need some advice." He heard a lot of background noise and then heard Bob yell, "Shut that door – I can't hear a thing."

"Sorry, Rock. It's like a circus around here. Did I hear

you say you need some advice? It's gonna cost ya!"

"If I had to pay you for all the legal advice you've given me over the last few years, I'd be flat broke."

"Yeah, you might have to mortgage the house. Oh, I forgot you don't have a house. It belongs to the church." They both laughed.

Robert Clayton was the official unpaid attorney for the church – a member of the church since he was a small boy, he felt like he owed the church something more than his tithe. His expertise in legal matters was a talent and his talents were in high demand. "Speak to me, Rev Rock, I've got to be in court in an hour."

Before the hour was up, Rock found himself waiting at the courthouse to be seen by the presiding judge. Rock had already been trained as a guardian-ad-litem and had served as one many times for the Department of Social Services. Several times he had been appointed by the court to represent children in divorce cases where custody was an issue, but he had also been assigned to represent one older adult who was not capable of handling his own affairs. Dr. Braem had suggested that in order to get information on Holly's condition, someone would need to have the right to make medical decisions for her. Bob suggested that while he was at it, he should also include Abigail in this petition. If he didn't do it soon, Social Services would appoint someone else and it would be much better for one person who would have connections to each of them and would have both of their interests at heart.

Bob's paralegal had worked up the papers in a flash

and together they caught the judge in his chambers before Bob's court case.

"Just like that?" Rock said with some surprise.

"Yep, just like that!"

Rock admired Bob's quick action. He had never let him down. "I suppose since I don't have ownership of a house, I'll have to mortgage my truck."

Bob laughed, "I just hope I don't ever have to collect on it!"

"Ahh, you can't judge it by its looks - it's a good old truck."

Back at his office, Rock made a list of questions he wanted to ask Dr. Braem. He put the guardian ad litem papers in a folder along with his notes and then checked his phone messages. There was one from Rebecca telling him that Abby had done well today, but was still asking questions about her mother. "She asked about you Rock. I think she took a liking to you. Call me tomorrow with any updates so I can relay them to Abby."

The next message was from Edie Mosher's son asking him if he could come by to see his mother one day soon. He had been meaning to, but somehow kept putting it on the back burner. She was his most difficult congregant with never a kind word to say about anyone.

"Lord, give me strength to deal with Miss Edie," he said as he got up and retrieved Reva's chicken and dumplings from the refrigerator. He was starved - the ham biscuit was long gone. I'll share this with Theo, he thought as he closed the office door behind him.

The next morning, Rock got to the hospital just in time to see Carly and Rob Higgins as they were checking out. Carly was nineteen - just a child herself and was complaining about having to go home so soon. "Y'all just herd us out like sheep," she said to the neonatal nurse. "How am I supposed to take care of this baby when I'm feeling so bad?"

"Honey, I'm sorry, but you just do what the rest of us do. Rob will help you out for a few days with changing diapers and housecleaning, won't you Rob?" Rob looked like he wanted a hole to open up in the floor and swallow him.

Rock chimed in, "I'm sure some of the women of the church will come around with some food. Rob, you just offer to let them hold the little one and it'll be all over - they'll be staying with you all day. There's just something about women and newborn babies - it's a sight to behold." Rob visibly perked up.

He took the stairs down to Pete's office. The door was open and he walked in. Pete put on his reading glasses and took a look at the papers. "This is good...." He hesitated. "Rock, I don't know where to start. I guess you could say the news is good and bad."

From the expression on his face, Rock knew something was wrong. "What do you mean?"

Peter Braem looked at the screen on his laptop. "I'll give you the good news first. Holly had a serious head injury, a broken ankle and a broken pelvis."

"That's not very good news," Rock said, but Dr. Braem kept talking.

"We induced a coma to reduce the amount of energy

the brain needs. As the brain starts healing and the swelling recedes, we can decrease the medication and she will come out of the coma. It's early to determine, but I'm optimistic that there will be no permanent impairment. There's always a chance that she'll have some memory loss, but with time, injuries like this almost always have a good outcome."

Rock sighed a breath of relief. "Ah, that is good news. How long will she be in this medically induced coma?"

"Each patient is different, but some patients have been kept in a coma for up to six months. I don't anticipate this being over a month - it just depends on how fast it heals."

"That long? I had no idea."

"But now for the bad news. Holly has had a double mastectomy in the last year." He waited for a moment for this news to sink in. Rock rubbed his forehead and shook his head.

"But Pete, she's so young!"

"Rock, breast cancer is not age or gender discriminate. It's uncommon, but even pre-adolescent girls have been diagnosed with breast cancer. You always hear that early detection is the key but most doctors don't recommend mammograms for women until about age fifty. And even though it's been emphasized for years, younger women don't always do self-examinations for breast lumps and by the time other symptoms appear, it's gone pretty far up the ladder in seriousness. I put Holly's name in the medical computer base once she was stabilized on Monday night and I've found something else very disturbing on her medical record."

Rock waited for him to continue. "I talked to her oncologist in Akron late yesterday and he told me that Holly's cancer has metastasized and is now on her left kidney and there's a small tumor on the frontal lobe of her brain. The two of them had discussed the treatment options and Dr. Wang had expressed his optimism to her. He suggested a round of chemo before removing the kidney - and then surgery along with radiation on the brain tumor. He felt it could very well save her life. But listen to this; Holly had decided not to undergo any more treatments. She told him she didn't want to go through all that and then just die anyway."

Rock looked incredulous. Dr. Braem went on. "And because it's an aggressive form of cancer, he says without treatment Holly has maybe six months or so to live. With the setback of this accident, she may not live that long. And there's more, Rock. Dr. Wang is the same oncologist who treated her mother for breast cancer. She died seven years ago when Holly was in college. This young woman's life has been full of adversities. She told Dr. Wang that her father is still alive but has dementia and is in a nursing facility. He doesn't even know her. She's had quite a life, hasn't she?"

Rock shook his head in disbelief. "Pete, why would she refuse treatment? Is she not thinking about the welfare of her child?"

"She had a pretty rough time with the chemo last year when they were trying to shrink the tumors before the breast surgery. She was deathly sick, Dr. Wang told me. And I'm sure she's aware that since the cancer came back, she may have to continue to just put out fires for the rest of her life, however long that may be. But also, it's his opinion, and mine, that the brain tumor may have affected her reasoning skills. The frontal lobe controls emotions and personality and even though it's not a large tumor yet, it still has the capability of affecting the thought process. I sure would like the opportunity to talk with her more about her treatment options. I'm not sure how many more years we could give her - or what her quality of life would be, but I would think she would want to fight for her life for that little girl of hers."

Rock walked over to the bookshelf and looked up at the picture. He was thinking of another young woman - the girl with violet eyes who would have given anything for a second chance. "Pete, is this your sailboat?"

"No, but it's a dream of mine to own one someday. I don't know when I would have time to sail though."

Rock nodded his head. "You know Pete, it's times like this that I'd like to sail off into the sunset and not have to deal with bad news anymore. This poor woman; she's had to deal with this all by herself and you know she must have been worried about what's going to happen to Abby. The strange thing is that Chief Hamilton found a South Carolina map in her car, with Park Place circled in red. Maybe she has some distant relatives around here someplace; and where is Abby's father? I'll go over to the Chief's office right now and tell him what you've found out through her medical records and your conversation with the oncologist in Columbus.

CHAPTER 6

Rock waited for Jess Hamilton, Park Place's police chief to finish giving instructions to one of his officers. "Come on in, Rev Rock and have a seat." He got up out of his chair to greet him and closed the door before they both sat down. Rock relayed Peter Braem's information without revealing too much of Holly Spencer's private medical history.

"This is good to know," said Jess. "You've filled in some major gaps. The Columbus Police Department sent out an officer yesterday to the address listed on Miss Spencer's driver's license. He talked to several of her neighbors." The buzzer rang on his phone. Jess picked it up and asked the dispatcher to hold his calls.

"The neighbors said that Holly had moved back into her father's home after her mother died. Shortly before she graduated from the university, she gave birth to Abby but never mentioned the child's father. When asked, she would clam up so they didn't push it. Abby's babysitter was a neighbor who has small children of her own. The neighbors love Abby and Holly and were very good to her while she was undergoing chemotherapy. They shocked last week when she told them she was taking Abby and would be gone for a while without offering them any further information. They must not have known about the new cancer."

Rock sat back in his chair. "So no one knows who Abby's father is?" Jess shook his head.

"Not yet. Their police department is very cooperative and they've offered to request Abby's birth records from the Clerk of Court. It may be a few days, but I'm hoping it will turn up something. We're pretty sure that Holly Spencer was not just passing through Park Place. She had arranged for a room for ten days over at the Holiday Inn at Exit 47 off the interstate. But we can't ask her because she hasn't said one word since the accident."

"Well that's not exactly true," said Rock. "She did say one word."

Jess looked doubtful. "What do you mean?"

"When I talked to Lonnie Welch yesterday, he said that despite the horrific rainstorm while he was getting her out of the car, she kept repeating the word *sunny* over and over. And then she lost consciousness."

"Lonnie didn't tell me that," Jess looked concerned.

"He only remembered it after I questioned him about anything she might have said. Do you think it means anything?"

"Unless she wasn't talking about the weather, and it doesn't make much sense that she would talk about sunny weather in a thunderstorm. The word *sunny* could also be spelled like the name, Sonny.

"Hmm...I hadn't thought about that. Do you know of any Sonny's here abouts?"

"The South is full of Sonny's, Rock. There's almost as many as there are Bubbas and Juniors." They both laughed.

"That's true," said Rock. "But most of the time only the immediate family use it and it's used a lot like Junior. When a boy is named after his father, it's a way of separating their identities within the family. Instead of Paul and Paul Jr., they call the the boy Sonny, or Junior. What do you think, Jess? Do you suppose Abby's father's name is Sonny and he lives somewhere in the area?"

"It's a long shot but it's worth looking into. We're shorthanded right now with one of our detectives on vacation. I could use some help tracking down Sonny's."

"I'm on it," Rock said as he got up from his chair. He was beginning to feel a little like Columbo.

CHAPTER 7

Rock parked his truck in his driveway and got out. He looked at his watch and saw it was already 4 p.m. He walked behind the manse and kept going past the office. He noticed that the grass was high because of the recent rains, but it would have to wait until later in the week when the landscapers came by to mow. The azaleas were holding on to a few late blooms and the rhododendrons were just beginning to bud. Jake Whitson had planted them a few years back amidst cries that he was wasting his time because it was too hot in Park Place for rhododendrons to flourish, but flourish they did. Jake had a small greenhouse behind his garage and he propagated camellias, rhododendrons, azaleas and anything else he could break a twig off a plant and get to grow.

As he reached the little cottage that had been his home before moving into the big house, he noticed that the roses on the trellis were beginning to bloom. He reached up to pick one and then walked up the steps and knocked on the door. He heard a familiar voice.

"Come on in Rock." Liz had just got in from work and was slipping off her jacket and shoes. "These shoes are the first things to go when I walk in this house," she said as she put her bags and file folders on the bench of the hall tree in the foyer. She tossed her shoes in the general area of the bedroom and draped her jacket over the back of a chair. "You want a glass of tea?" she asked making her way back to the kitchen. Rock followed her and handed her the rose.

"Have I ever turned down your iced tea?"

"Not that I recall," she said as she put the flower in a bud vase and then breathed in the fragrance. "Ahh - the first roses always smell the best." She put the vase on the table, pulled out two glasses and opened the refrigerator door.

When the church had sold the cottage, Rock had met the couple and took an immediate liking to them. Ron Logan was the CEO of a manufacturing plant that had just been built in the business park near the interstate. His wife Liz was a high school guidance counselor and found a job right away at the new high school. They had just moved from Atlanta and they were Southern born and bred. Not surprisingly, they had a lot in common. Not that he didn't have things in common with his friends from the North. There were many of them now due to the close proximity to Charlotte and the growing job market there. Sun's Up Retirement Village had also brought in an abundance of snowbirds looking to settle in a milder climate. Many of them had joined Park Place Presbyterian and had been a blessing in the life and works of the church.

He and Ron had become good friends and played golf and fished in nearby farm ponds on Saturdays. Ron and Liz had joined the Methodist Church down the street which was nice because he found it hard to be anything other than the spiritual leader of his congregants least they think he was playing favorites by forming close friendships with just a few. As they got to know each other, the three of them went out to dinner and spent a good bit of time together. They invited him up to their house in the mountains on his vacation weekends and he loved it. Their deck was built out over a little mountain stream and Liz would sit out on it and watch as the two of them donned their fishing vests and felt-soled boots and made their way walking on the rocks in the stream fishing for trout. "You boys look like something out of Field and Stream Magazine," she teased. They would bring their catch in and Ron would deep-fry the trout as Rock and Liz set the table and made the side dishes.

All that came to an abrupt halt two years ago when Ron had a massive heart attack while sitting in a board meeting at work and died in the ambulance on the way to the hospital. He was only forty-four – two years Rock's senior. Liz had been devastated. They had never had children and Ron was her whole life. She was only in her early thirties at the time and had not quite given up on starting a family even though they had been married for ten years. They had even talked about adoption, but had not started the process yet.

Rock was a big consolation to Liz as she went through the difficult days ahead. He had helped her through probate court and had grieved right along with her. She knew how much Ron's friendship had meant to him and they both found it comforting to continue their relationship as friends eventually getting to the point of remembering with laughter some of the lighter moments the three of them had shared. They had settled now on a mutual respect and friendship that was comfortable and easy going. There had never been any thoughts of a romance between the two of them. Rock thought they had the best of both worlds. They were simply friends - no involvement and no entanglement - the two things that scared him to death.

Liz had made sandwiches while Rock sat at the table drinking his tea. "You haven't had dinner, have you? I skipped lunch today and I'm starved. Have one." Over the sandwiches, Rock told her about the mystery mom and the little girl with impeccable manners. "What can I do to help," she asked. "I knew you would say that," he answered and they took their tea out on the porch and talked about it until the sun got low in the sky.

CHAPTER 8

The week went by in a blur as it always did. Rock had a few leads on Sonny's in the area, but so far none had panned out. It was a beautiful Sunday morning with temperatures expected to be in the eighties later in the day. It was one of the last Sundays he could expect full attendance. School would be out in another week, Memorial Day was just around the corner, and his flock would be vacationing throughout the summer.

During the Liturgical readings, he looked out over his congregation and knew that he had lost some of them before he even began his sermon. Maura McCarthy had a pen and paper and seemed to be writing a list. Larry Braswell had settled in to the pew a little too comfortably. His wife would have to work double duty today to keep him from snoring.

Normally Maura was attentive. She took the liturgy readings to heart and read them with feeling. And she was one of the few that he could count on to fully understand his message. She was dependable – give her a task and she would follow it through to completion. Rock knew that he had put too much on her plate in the last while. There had been no volunteers for teaching Sunday School, so Maura had taken on a children's class. He had asked her to chair the Stewardship Committee four years ago and she had taken the bull by the horns. But, every time she tried to step down from the leadership role, he begged her to stay. She was also on the Building and

Planning Committee and thank God, she was there. If not, they would have been mired down by endless discussions, never making a decision when the need for building a new nursery came up. Maura kept them on track – the only woman among many men. She was a sweet and gentle soul, but she made one bold move that handled the testosterone-packed meeting in one of the planning sessions. He could see her frustration but never expected her to explode.

"I feel like we take one step forward and two steps back from one meeting to the next," she had said. "Things that we agree on at one meeting, you act as if it's a totally new concept at the next! I can't imagine what you guys are thinking! Whatever happened to faith that we can accomplish the tasks ahead of us? Has God ever let us down when we're in the midst of doing His will?" She had picked up her folders from the table as if to leave. "We're either going to make a decision that we can stick with tonight, or I'm going home. I have better things to do than spin my wheels."

Total silence followed her outburst. After a brief pause, the chairman cleared his throat and said, "Well boys, you heard what the lady said, let's get on with the show."

Maura's few words had accomplished what Rock had been trying to do for months. He had expected it to produce some grumblings by the men on the committee but to his surprise they were compliant. They even congratulated her for coming up with a plan to save money by remodeling rather than building an addition. By moving the wall in one of the largest rooms and utilizing the closet space in both rooms, they were able to work in the much-needed new nursery.

Maura's personal life was just as hectic as her church life. Her part time job at the library, a sick husband, her adult children and grandchildren all competed for her attention. Rock admonished himself for what he had done. Maura was like Mary and he had turned this Mary into a Martha. Mary had set at the Lord's feet and listened to what he was saying. Martha was so busy with preparations of food and cleaning that she had no time to listen. *"Martha, Martha,"* Jesus had said, *"You are worried and distracted by many things; Mary has chosen the better part, which will not be taken away from her."* Rock decided he would have to ease up on Maura - soon.

***

He continued the scanning of his flock as George read the announcements. Miss Edie Mosher was on the front pew fiddling with her cane. She had already disturbed several people in the row behind her as she dropped it on the floor and raked it around under her seat trying to find a place for it. Her otherwise attractive face was marred with her usual scowl and her mouth seemed to be turned down in a permanent frown. She was not growing old gracefully but with disdain and intolerance for every poor soul she met. She was a widow with only one grown son and Rock thought she must be lonely, but she could have had plenty of friends if she had not been so unpleasant. He knew he needed to put forth more of an effort to spend time with her, but his dread of dealing with her bitter nature kept him from doing more than a customary visit twice a year. And then she spent the whole time complaining that he didn't come around more often. Rats, he had forgotten to call her son back to set a time to visit. I'll go see her this week, he thought, knowing he would have to mentally prepare himself for the visit. He was startled out of his reverie when George announced, "Let us stand to sing Hymn number 426, *He Leadeth Me.*"

***

Crowder's Feed, Seed and Hardware Store had been in Junie Crowder's family for over 75 years. It had once been the hub of activity for farmers during planting season, but now that the chain stores had built on the outskirts of town, it produced just enough income to keep the doors open for Junie and Kathleen. They had thought about closing the business but it did help to supplement their Social Security. Kathleen told the ladies in her sewing club that she would fight tooth and nail to keep it open – even if she spent her last dime doing it. "I'm not having Junie Crawford right under my feet every minute," she had said. "Lord have mercy, he would drive me plumb crazy."

It wasn't on anybody's calendar, but on any given Monday morning at about ten o'clock, you could find a few locals gathering inside to talk and socialize. Larry Braswell's wife, Jenny, said it was worse than any beauty shop she had ever been in. She didn't hesitate to pick Larry's brain when he came home though. Men were much more naïve about spreading gossip than women.

Junie stood on the outside of the store surveying the construction paper sign he had taped to the window earlier. Large block letters written with a marker announced to passers-by - BIG CLOSEOUT SALE TODAY - PARKS WHOOPER TOMATO PLANTS - $1.00 EACH. "Dadgummit," he complained to himself. "I put two O's instead of two P's in WHOPPER. Ain't no wonder nobody's been in - who ever heard of a Parks Whooper tomato?" He stood on the step ladder, pulled down the sign and marked over the second letter O and made it into a letter P. There, he thought, a little sloppy, but at least they know I can spell.

It was nigh on ten o'clock and the only paying customer in so far had been Maura and Danny McCarthy's granddaughter. Emily had been saving her allowance doing chores for her Nana and had walked in the door with a $10 bill and a $5 bill in her hand. He saw Maura waiting in the car at the curb. He had a feeling she was here to buy the Appaloosa Breyer Horse she kept eyeing every time she came in the store with Danny. When Junie saw how much money she had, he hurried and marked it down 10% from the $15 price tag so she would have enough to pay the sales tax. She walked out carrying the box with a smile on her face and a little bit of change in her pocket.

He walked to the back of the store where the others were talking. There were three bags of feed sitting at the end of Aisle number 3, the horse tack aisle. This was the least busy aisle in the store since the new tack shop down the street had drawn away some of his horse farm customers. Aisle 3 held horse blankets, bits, riding breeches and horse grooming supplies. Rev Rock was sitting on the Feed-Rite horse food bag; Larry Braswell sat on the Chicken Scratch and the dog food bag was, at the present time, unoccupied. Its usual occupant was busy storming around the store.

"Where's the bag of Old Roy?" Fred Laney fumed.

"I sold it Saturday. Quit yer fussin' and sit on that Purina bag I pulled out for you," Junie said.

"Yeah," Larry chipped in, "Purina's more expensive. You'll think you've got the King's throne - it'll go to your head if you're not careful."

***

Rock watched his friends banter back and forth. Fred's Barber Shop was closed on Mondays and for the past two years the four friends met at Junie's store over a Cheerwine and a pack of peanuts and re-hashed their weekend.

"Junie, you know I had just got the Old Roy all smashed down nice and comfortable and you up and sold it!"

I've got some more on back-order - just beat on that Purina a little bit and it'll fit your butt just fine. I'm surprised anyone bought the Old Roy with it all crushed up like it was."

Rock had come in a little early to ask about Kathleen but everyone else had come in early too. She was to go into the hospital for tests on Friday and Rock knew that Junie's nervous energy this morning was a result of his worrying about her. He finally sat down in his old straight back chair and turned to Rock. "Rev Rock, I gotta' ask you something," he said. "You know that Bible verse about three or more people prayin' for something? Well, would ya' mind prayin' for my Kathleen?" Rock was touched by the older man's sincerity. Kathleen was in the Baptist Church every time the doors were open, but as far as Rock knew, Junie had never belonged to a church.

"Matthew 19:20, *For where two or three are gathered together in my name, there am I in the midst of them.*"

"That's it," said Junie. Rock put one hand on Junie's shoulder and the other on Larry's. Fred joined in by reaching out to Junie on the other side. "Lord, you gave us a promise and we're holding you to it. We are gathering together in your name today knowing that you're in our midst. Hear our prayer and give comfort and healing to Junie and Kathleen." Junie didn't hear much else. He just felt a sense of peace settling over him that he didn't have before.

***

Jamie was on duty again when Rock walked past the nurses' station. "Mr. Lattimore asked if you had been here yet this morning, Rev Rock. I think he's expecting a visit from his preacher." Ned had been admitted right after church yesterday with chest pains, but it had turned out to be a gallbladder attack.

"Thanks Jamie, that's why I came by. Is the surgery still scheduled for this afternoon?"

"Yes, it'll be a couple of hours before he's prepped

and ready to go. After you see him, stop back by. Dr. Braem is making his rounds right now, but he asked me to come find him if you came in."

After Rock visited and prayed with the Lattimore family, he stopped by Peter's office. "Rock, I've asked an oncologist from Charlotte to come by next week to evaluate Miss Spencer. Can you meet with us afterwards?"

"Just call me with the details and I'll be here. How is she today?"

"I thought I would try weaning her off some of the meds that we're using to sedate her but we did another MRI yesterday and there's still some intracranial pressure. I'm going to leave things as they are for now. You can stop by to see her on your way out. She has a visitor."

A visitor? Rock wondered who could be visiting, but when he walked in the door, he smiled. Betty Ann Williams was sitting by Holly's bed knitting a pink shawl. "Do you think she'll like it?" she asked.

"She'll love it!" he said. Betty Ann was the mission coordinator for the Presbyterian Women and Rock knew if she had her way, there would be a steady flow of visitors to see the young woman who had no family.

***

He had dropped by the cottage to give Liz a box of teabags. It was the least he could do since he was always drinking her tea. He forgot it was her reading club night so he just left them on the porch in the rocker he always sat in and walked back to his house. Theo was waiting when he walked in with a bag of groceries. He had bought a catnip toy mouse and Theo started batting it around on the floor. He fixed a sandwich and a glass of iced water and headed for his armchair. He read for a few minutes and was out like a light. He barely remembered getting undressed and going to bed. Theo was not consigned to the laundry room and took full advantage by sleeping without making a sound on the other side of the bed. He had learned by now that if he didn't make any noise all night, he wouldn't be thrown out.

CHAPTER 9

"No!" Maura knew instantly it was her own scream that woke her as she lay in the four-poster bed where she had slept almost every night of her sixty-seven years. The impact of the scene that had been the subject of her nightmare was the same scene that had haunted her dreams many nights over the years. It had been frozen in her memory since the morning she turned four on November 1st 1948. She knew now that Jim had not thought about it being her birthday when he did what he did.

Maura had awakened early that morning to the smell of bacon frying and ran into the kitchen. Momma was busy with breakfast and Daddy was at the table reading the newspaper and drinking his coffee. "Please daddy, will you put some cheese in your coffee?"

He pinched Maura's cheek and smiled while spooning out hot melting cheese from his coffee. "I've already done it, birthday girl" and spooned it right into Maura's waiting mouth. It was her favorite part of breakfast.

Momma finished setting the table and said, "Now be a big girl and wake up that lazy brother of yours. Lloyd will be here in fifteen minutes to pick him up for work and I haven't heard him stir about yet."

It wasn't often that Maura got up before Jim so she ran into his room calling "Jimmy, Jimmy did you know I'm a birthday girl." A four-year-old has trouble comprehending death, but seeing the odd pallor of Jim's skin and the limp body hanging from the rafters produced a scream that had forever lived in her ears. Her gentle brother, the reluctant war hero, had decided he could no longer live with the atrocities he had seen and the lives he had been forced to take while on the war front in France and then Germany.

The clock said 5:14 a.m. Maura rolled over, turned the pillow for the cool side and tried to go back to sleep. At 5:36 she gave up and shuffled into the bathroom and then downstairs to the kitchen to start the coffee. This was the time of morning Maura savored. She had at least an hour before Danny would wake and want breakfast. She heard the soothing sound of "hummmmm ..... chi ..... hummmmm .....chi" coming from the tank outside the guestroom which had become Danny's bedroom during the times his illness prevented him from climbing stairs. It was the sound of life, an almost musical sound like breath itself that provided oxygen for her husband of almost 50 years. His emphysema had been caused from years of smoking and although she knew that it had been a terrible addiction for him to fight, she still resented what it had taken away from them. They had put back a little money here and there and Danny had once said that they would take a full year and just throw darts at a North American map and go from place to place wherever it landed. Now he had limitations, and always needed to be near an oxygen tank whether driving or working ouside.

Maura took her coffee outside on the screened porch where she could enjoy the crisp Spring morning air. She waved as she saw Rock backing out of his driveway. She walked to the screen door when she saw that he had stopped and rolled down his window. "How's Danny doing since he got out of the hospital?" Maura just smiled and shrugged and saw the understanding in Rock's eyes. "Come over if you need a shoulder" and she knew that he meant it. She also knew that he felt guilty for the amount of work he had asked her to do in the church. She had been meaning to go over and tell him that she loved doing the work of the church, no matter how much she fretted and fussed. It was the only thing that pulled her out of the downward spiral of depression that engulfed her when Danny was sick.

Maura walked back in the house. She loved this old house that held so many memories of her childhood. She and Danny had moved back into it when she had inherited it, just as her mother had inherited it before her. Each had made a few cosmetic changes. Her parents had lowered the ten-foot-high ceilings by installing block tiles. "Too high to get up there and paint," her father had reasoned. Maura and Danny had taken it all down when they moved in and restored it to its original beadboard.

The kitchen had been remodeled twice over the years, keeping its vintage appeal but with modern appliances. The outside still maintained the late 19th century charm that graced so many of the homes in Park Place. As Maura walked by the large dining room fireplace, she heard an all too familiar sound from the past. At this very spot, family members would occasionally hear the sounds of a two-way conversation of ham radio operators. One of the voices was of her gentle brother, Jim whose hobby had been the only joy in his life after he came home from the war. But the joy had not been enough. Oddly enough it would be these sounds that would comfort her mother and father long after Jim was gone. Some said it was his ghost, but Maura knew that it was just a sweet memory – one that he had left them to somehow drown out the screams in the night. She picked up the little figural music box on the mantle. It had been a gift from Jim. She turned it on its base several turns and the little Dutch girl spun around as the melody played. She was humming along with the music as she walked down the hallway.

"Honey, where are you?" Maura felt a tenderness wash over her for this man that she had pledged to love 'in sickness and in health' for as long as she lived. With renewed strength, she headed back to the kitchen. "I've got coffee ready. I'll bring it to you." As she sat it on the tray beside his bed, he reached over to kiss her and she saw the shame and regret flit across his face. What have I done to this sweet man, she thought. Have I worn my resentment on my sleeve and made him feel guilty about his illness? With a quick kiss back, she vowed to make the most of every minute she had with Danny. They would continue to make good memories in the old house that had been touched by sadness but had also been infused with much happiness.

***

Rock walked out the kitchen door and across the courtyard to the office. The air was crisp and clear. A cold front had come in overnight and the forecast was for temps in the upper seventies - quite a change from the 86-degree high from the day before. The change of seasons in the Carolinas always held a few surprises and this late May cool spell was one of them. Reva was on the phone when Rock walked in. The office smelled like cinnamon buns and coffee. Rock followed his nose to the coffee pot and a casserole dish beside it. He opened the lid and the smell alone was enough to make him smile. Six fresh baked pastries were staring him in the face and they were still steaming. He got Reva's attention by holding the lid up in the air and pointing to the dish. "Are these for me," he mouthed. She waved him off but nodded. He poured a cup of coffee and put one of the cinnamon rolls on a paper plate on the counter.

"He just walked in Jess." She put the phone on hold. "It's Jess Hamilton - something about having a lead for you." He took his first bite and picked up the phone.

"You're interrupting something good here," he mumbled with his mouth full. "Reva's feeding me again. Okay, I'll follow up on it - just give me directions."

Jess had remembered that Jack Haywood had a grandson named Sonny who had lived with them a while. He had lived up North somewhere before moving in with Jack so it might be worth following up on. "They live out in the middle of nowhere," Jess said. "But I've got directions. Stop by and talk with me a while. These directions are too complicated to give over the phone."

Rock grabbed another cinnamon bun and gave Reva a salute. "Don't eat them all while I'm gone," he said and walked out the door. As he backed out of the driveway, he saw Maura on her porch. He asked about Danny and chatted with her for a minute before moving on.

***

Jess was in his office when he got there. Rock relayed to him Peter Braem's latest report about Holly when Jess inquired about her condition. "I'll let Rebecca know - I don't know what she'll tell Abby. I'm sure the poor child thinks it's normal for her mom to be sick. It hasn't been all that long ago that she had her surgeries, has it?"

"Not so long that she wouldn't remember," said Rock. "I've been meaning to ask if you've received Abby's birth certificate yet?"

"We have, and I wish I could tell you that it revealed her father's name, but it doesn't. That box was left blank on the certificate - so our mystery continues."

No father listed, thought Rock, and she would have no mother if her cancer was left untreated. A few minutes later he left Jess' office with a crude map and was on his way to the 'middle of nowhere' as Jess had called it.

CHAPTER 10

*H*ere *I am! I stand at the door and knock. If anyone hears my voice and opens the door, I will come in and eat with him, and he with me.*

~Revelation 3:20

Rock was beginning to think he was lost. The narrow path on the power line right-of-way rambled on and on through little scrubby pines that were scratching the sides of the truck. Rock looked for a place to turn around, but it was straight ahead or nothing. He looked at his directions again and plowed on. Moss covered rocks lined one side and a few scraggly hardwoods leaned here and there making a crisscross pattern through the cut-over. He had learned about cut-overs from Mary Jo Hilton. They were driving to Charlotte for lunch and Rock had commented on a piece of property that looked desolate. "Why don't they just bulldoze it all down instead of leaving it so haphazard?" he had remarked. "This is the way they harvest the Loblolly pine thickets" she had answered. "The scraggly looking hardwoods will someday right themselves and grow up toward the sun with no tall pines to stunt their growth. The tall straight pine trees are used for lumber and the others are hauled across the river to the pulpwood plant. The pulpwood is used for paper production and to make OSB boards for construction."

"Do they replant the pines?" he asked.

"Most of the time they use seeds or seedlings to replant. The seedlings are small so it gives the hardwoods time to grow bigger and then they're harvested - but sometimes they just let them naturally regenerate." She knew a lot about pines. Come to think of it, Mary Jo knew a lot about everything and if she didn't, she made it up along the way. And no matter what, she had to have the last word. Adding insult to injury, she always had to drive her fancy car while he sat meekly in the passenger seat. As he drove, the list of Mary Jo's faults grew longer. Yes, he was glad he got out while the gettin' was good!

By now he had left the cut-over behind and the driveway improved some along with the scenery. Finally, there were some small trees and shrubs lining the driveway as it made its way parallel to the right-of-way. Remnants of an old chimney were visible across a little patch of woods – a large chimney where a large plantation home had once stood – now in ruins. Rock braked suddenly. About 30 feet off the road, he spotted what looked like a gravestone. He loved old gravestones about as well as he loved old houses and porches and rockers and.....well, just about everything old. He got out of the truck and walked the short distance to the gravestone. *HENRY CROWE – died 1936 – age 72.* This was a nice stone standing about chest high and engraved with dogwood blossoms. Right beside it was a dogwood tree that looked as if it had been planted a number of years – more than likely planted right after Henry Crowe had been planted, thought Rock, knowing that it was a Southern custom to plant pretty flowering trees in a cemetery beside a loved one's grave. Thinking it improbable that just one grave would be there, he scouted around for more. About 20 feet away was a more primitive headstone. *OUR BELOVED MOTHER – JULIA CROWE – DIED 1920 - AGE 82.* Raking leaves away with his foot, another small stone lay broken and scattered near Henry Crowe. It said simply O. W. These initials had been hand carved, unlike the two professionally carved stones. These could be the gravestones of former slaves of the plantation owner and their descendants. They may have lived on the plantation long after they were freed - share-cropping or continuing to work for the plantation family in much the same manner as they had when they were slaves. Many of the slaves in this part of the south had nowhere to go when they were freed and some had been treated with kindness by their owners and stayed on out of necessity, earning whatever they could pay them. Many more had suffered at the hands of their masters and moved to the North where there were more jobs to be had. There may have been more gravestones if he had time to unearth them, but he would come back, he thought, when he had more time. Liz would like this, he thought.

As he got deeper in the woods, he thought he could smell wood smoke. He rounded a short bend in the road and came abruptly upon a single-wide trailer. In the front yard, there was a black and tan coonhound on the end of a long chain soaking in the warm sun on top of a doghouse. When he saw Rock, he began to howl in the way coonhounds do. I hope this is the only dog they have, thought Rock, stepping out of the truck and watching his back. He left the driver's side door open in case he had to make a mad dash back into it.

The trailer had been roofed over and there was a small room addition from hence came the smoke from a small chimney. A narrow gravel walkway led to the front door. Large clumps of Pampas grass were growing on either side of the walkway. The grass looked as if it had never been cut back and was as tall as the trailer. Rock noticed the bottle tree in front of the picture window of the trailer. His grandmother had used a bottle tree for drying her canning jars, but he had heard the stories that people once used them as a means of protecting their homes by trapping evil spirits within the colorful bottles. This one was an old cedar tree with all the branches stripped, and wine bottles of every color pointing down with their lips around the nubs that were left of the branches. The thought of the evil "spirits" that had been contained in these cheap wine bottles was enough to make Rock's stomach churn. He had visions of a Boone's Farm moment from back in his early college days.

Reva had called the Haywoods to tell them Rock was coming for a visit. Eva Haywood met Rock at the door as if she had been waiting on this very moment all her life. She was a little bent and held onto her cane as if it was another limb, but otherwise seemed fit and alert. She had on a mint green polyester pantsuit that was still holding its own after close to a half century of wear. "Jack, looky who's here – it's 'at preacher from over to the Presbyteery Church – come on in preacher – ain't no use to wait out in th' cold."

Cold? Rock smiled. It was an unseasonably cool morning, but not cold. He stepped into a tidy living room filled with an eclectic mix of flea market furniture and pictures on the wall. It was paneled in a dark red cedar paneling. A wood burning stove was at one end of the room and was putting out a lot of heat. A little too much, thought Rock as he took off his jacket.

The room addition had been well thought out. It was used as their living room. The former living room was now used as a dining area and opened up into the kitchen giving it a much roomier look. A large oak table was in the center surrounded by a hodgepodge of mismatched chairs. A chest type freezer, a washer and a dryer took up one wall. Shelves had been built above them to hold cleaning supplies and an ironing board was propped in the corner. Every space was utilized, but it was neat and clean.

A wonderful aroma filled the room and Rock commented on it. "It's a big ole pot of pinto beans with some streak o' lean cookin' on top o' the wood stove over there. It'll be done in a little if you want to eat with us. I got some fresh cornbread and a glass of milk I can offer you too. It's been a coon's age since we had a preacher eat with us and we could sure use some extra blessin' right now." Rock knew she was serious and he found it hard to turn down a home cooked meal. "Well, I guess I could stay for a bite if you're sure it won't inconvenience you," he said.

"Jack, set an extra chair – we got us a preacher joinin' us for dinner!"

While Eva was setting the table, Rock sat in her recliner and tried to make small talk with Jack. He had tried talking to him before at the Feed and Seed, but always felt like he was carrying on a one-sided conversation. This time wasn't any better.

"Jack, do you have any other family around here?"

"Yes sir."

"Oh? Brothers – sisters – children?"

"Got a brother." It was pure monotone.

"Does he live in Park Place or close by?"

"Over in Lancaster."

This was going nowhere. Maybe he would have better luck with Eva. Jack was just one of those people that you had to labor over a conversation with. Eva called out from the kitchen, "Come on boys, soup's on." Rock realized he was hungry. Reva's pastries had run out of steam.

"Our heavenly Father, we ask You to bless this house and the ones who live here. I thank You Lord for Eva and Jack and for their generosity in sharing their table. Bless this food to the nourishment of our bodies and bless the hands that prepared it. May the words of our lips spring forth from hearts of gratitude and may we be a blessing to each other as we fellowship today. Through Christ our Lord we pray. Amen."

Rock had never met Eva until today. "Miss Eva, if I had known you were such a good cook, I would have made your acquaintance before now," Rock said as he pushed back his chair from the table. "But if I ate with you often, I'd have to let my belt out a notch." Eva blushed and busied herself scraping the dishes into a bucket that Rock intuitively knew would be the dog's supper tonight.

"We enjoyed your company, preacher. We thank you

for blessing our food the way you did. It seems to mean more coming from a preacher and all."

"No Ma'am, God hears your prayers just as much as he hears mine. That's his promise."

"I don't know – it just seems like you preachers must have a direct line to the Almighty. Me and old Jack here – now it seems like we're on a party line or something – like it's hard to get through to Him and like He ain't listenin' to us when we do. It ain't every day we get to share our table, livin' way out here and all. We don't have many passers-by, if you know what I mean." Rock smiled. He couldn't imagine anyone voluntarily driving down that rutted driveway unless they had to. If there wasn't a mailbox at the end of the drive, you would never know there was a house here. He got up and started drying the dishes as Eva washed them.

"Miss Eva, I know you have some family that has moved away from here. Do you ever hear from them?" Rock thought he had better get to the point while he had Eva's undivided attention.

"You must be talkin' about my boy Nathan who moved up north when he graduated from Clemson. He always was a smart one, he was. He got him some big fancy job up in Maryland and married a Yankee woman and we don't see or hear much from him anymore. He sent his boy – Sonny we call him - down here to live with us when he got in some trouble in college, but he stole Jack's truck and run away after a few months. Said he couldn't live back here in the sticks. They found Jack's truck up in Charlotte in a drug neighborhood and the sheriff took Jack up there and picked it up."

"The boy was just ruined by his mama and daddy, is what it was Preacher. He never had to work for nothin' – they gave him everything he wanted. We hadn't heard anything from him since he took Jack's truck, but Nathan called a while back and said Sonny had called him asking for a loan to put down a deposit on an apartment. He's trying to get away from the bunch he's been hanging out with. He's over in Sparta and he's got him two part-time jobs – one at a motorcycle shop and the other at a livestock auction. He said he's kicked his habit and working right steady - said if we ever needed to get in touch with him, he could be reached over at the livestock auction over there and he gave us the phone number. We been wantin' to go see him, but Jack's old truck ain't dependable enough to get us over there and back – I was hoping he would come to see us. I sure would like to see that boy straightened up. He's going on 30 years old and it's about time for him to shape up like a man."

That's not much, thought Rock. But it was more than he had. He figured it for a dead end, but would check it out just the same. He pulled out a card from his wallet. "Miss Eva, call me sometime when you feel up for a drive in the country. I'll drive you and Jack over to Sparta to see your grandson sometime if you wish." "Why preacher, that shore would be nice. You come back and eat with us any time, you hear?" He knew she meant it.

Rock walked back through the living room to say goodbye to Jack, but he was snoring like a bear in his recliner with "The Young and the Restless" blaring from the TV. "Thank you for the hospitality, Jack," he said to unhearing ears. He let himself out the door, walked past the howling hound and saw that he had forgot to come back and close the truck door. Battery, please don't be dead, he thought. Triple A would have a hard time finding me back here. He turned the key in the ignition. It cranked right up. He patted the dashboard. "I knew I could depend on you," he said out loud and made his way with much caution back down the driveway.

CHAPTER 11

"**D**og-gonit! I shouldn't have bragged on you." Steam was pouring from under the truck's hood. He looked at the temperature gauge and it was as far as it could go on HOT. Rock was by no means a mechanic, but he knew he needed to pull over. The Piggly Wiggly was just ahead and he pulled into the parking lot. He got out and opened the hood to check the radiator. No way can I get that cap off, he thought and stood there feeling helpless as he watched steam spew into the air.

"Looks like you could use some help." Rock looked up and saw Ralph Huey's construction truck had pulled up beside him.

"I sure could," said Rock. "I think it's the radiator."

"Let it cool off a bit and I'll add some water to it. I've got plenty back here," he said, pointing to the large five-gallon water cooler on the back of his truck. As they waited, several people he knew drove by and honked their horns.

Lonnie Welch pulled up in the EMT van and got out. "You OK here?" he asked.

Rock looked around and saw that they were attracting even more attention now that Lonnie had driven up and he could see why: steam spouting out of his truck, Ralph hefting a big orange water cooler on his shoulders, and now and emergency vehicle pulled along beside them. This would probably make the Park Place Gazette's front page; there wasn't much else going on in town. He smiled at the thought.

"I'm fine," he said, "but I don't know about Old Faithful here. She just conked out on me."

"I'll stay until you get it going. Besides, I've got another joke for you."

"I could use a little humor right now."

"Well, you know Rev Rock - it's not politically correct to tell jokes about people of certain regions of the world anymore, so I'll just use the word fellers here."

"Now there were these two fellers, I'll name 'em Nemo an Jeff. Well, them fellers had got rich and they hired themselves a pilot to take them up in the air and give them some pilotin' lessons. After they had been up a while, the pilot, he up and died of a heart attack. Now those two boys had a little flying experience so they proceeded to looking for an airport to land in. 'I think I see one', Jeff said. "See all those planes down there?'.

'Yep', said Nemo. 'Let's see if we can land this thing. Hey, there's not much space to land on – can't be more than fifty or sixty feet of space. I'm gonna need your help. I'll pull up on the runway and as soon as I touch down, you pull back on this here brake, you understand'. He commenced to land the plane and all went well. When the wheels touched the pavement, Jeff pulled back hard and they skidded to a stop. 'Whew - that was close!' Nemo said. 'That was the shortest runway I've ever seen'.

'It sure was short' Jeff said. 'But it looks like it's about a mile wide'."

Rock and Ralph were still laughing twenty minutes later as they poured water into the cooled off radiator.

Rock got in and it cranked right up.

"Who's your mechanic?"

"Lee Robinson," Rock answered. "He knows this truck inside-out." Ralph got in his own truck and rolled down the window. "I'll follow you over there in case you have any more trouble."

"I think it's the thermostat," said Lee, as he lifted his head out from under the hood. "Or it could be the water pump or the intake. Thermostat's the least expensive of the three; it's sort of hit and miss with water leaks so let's go with the thermostat first. I'll send Billy over to the parts store and we'll have you back on the road again in about an hour."

True to his word, an hour later Lee slammed the hood. "Just check it now and again by adding water to the radiator. You'll be able to tell if it's leaking if it takes more than a quart. Bring it back if that doesn't solve the problem."

"Maybe it's time to trade it in."

Lee put his hands on his hips. "Now don't be doing that. We've fixed about everything that could go wrong with it and it's a fine old truck."

"That's a relief. I don't need a new truck payment. Besides, you wouldn't get any of my money if I bought a new one, would you?"

Lee smiled. "Ya' got that right."

CHAPTER 12

*A*nd pray for us, too, that God may open a door for our message, so that we may proclaim the mystery of Christ, for which I am in chains. Pray that I may proclaim it clearly, as I should.

~ Colossians 4: 3-4

After spending an hour of his Saturday morning at the Children's Home, Rock had come back to his study to work on his sermon. It was Memorial Day weekend and he knew several families that would be out of town, but it was also Pentecost Sunday and there were three new members joining the church. He had been holding new member classes for Joe and Maria Johnson who had recently moved from Connecticut, and RuthAnn Maxwell's new daughter-in-law was joining by transfer from Calvary Presbyterian in Charlotte.

He had never had problems preparing a Pentecost sermon. A quickening of his own spirit always preceded his reading of God's Word about the birthday of the Church – the day of the coming of the Holy Spirit on Jesus' earliest followers. Today had been a difficult day all around. It was becoming increasingly hard to explain to Abby about why she couldn't yet visit her mother. He had found himself avoiding making eye contact with her, until today. He had taken the children outside while Rebecca cleaned up the kitchen. Estelle had taken the morning off.

The weekday dorm counselors were handing off their duties to the weekend counselors. He sat on a long bench under the rose arbor while the children played on the swings and slides. Abby came and sat beside him and put her small hand in his. She looked up at him and he saw tears in her eyes. "Rev Rock," she said, "Am I ever going to see my mommy again?"

That did it. He didn't know how or when – and he didn't care what the social worker said about now not being the right time. Despite the apprehension of her seeing Holly's IV's and tubes, he was going to get that child in to see her mother.

It was restlessness rather than frustration that he felt. He knew his sermon would come to him as it always did. Early on, he had asked his faithful flock to pray for him each week as he prepared his sermons just as in the early church the Apostle Paul had asked the churches to pray for him that he would speak God's truth. Colossians 4: 3-4 was printed in the bulletin each week with a personal note from him requesting those prayers. Several people told him of their prayers, but more importantly, he felt them.

He got up from his chair and left the unfinished sermon on his desk. As he walked toward the manse, he noticed Liz sitting on her porch propped back in her rocker with her nose in the newspaper. A big pitcher of iced tea was on the small table at her side. That's what I need, he thought. He wasn't quite sure whether he meant the iced tea or the nice quiet companionship of his friend. She saw him then, and pointed to the tea pitcher. "Got plenty, come sit a spell."

He took the steps two at a time and felt a sense of peace and relaxation envelop him as soon as his feet hit the familiar planks on the porch. He looked up at the pale blue ceiling. When Rock had first moved into this house, the old tongue and groove ceiling had at least three coats of paint that was chipping and flaking. He had taken it upon himself to strip it down to the original finish and then primed and painted it a pale blue. "Haint blue," one of his church members had said. He hadn't heard the term before, but she told him the story. Blue porch ceilings had originated in South Carolina by African descendents and it was their way of thinking that ghosts or 'haints' would not cross water and the color of blue would trick the ghosts into turning away from the threshold of the house. The trick was a myth, he thought, because many an old house held its fair share of ghosts.

The soft blue that Rock had chosen for the ceiling was the hue of the Carolina sky and it always soothed his soul. The air was fragrant with the sweet scent of the small white flowers on the Confederate Jasmine that was growing on the trellis beside the roses.

"You know Liz, sometimes I wish the church hadn't built the new manse. I miss this old house – I miss this porch and these flowers – I just miss everything about it. I putter around in those big rooms feeling like I'm talking to an echo."

"I think they thought you were going to marry and have a big family." There was silence but Liz plowed on. She wanted to know.

"Well, why didn't you get married? I know there's not a shortage of women in Park Place."

"I don't know- it just didn't happen."

Liz laughed, "Hmm, you make it sound like marriage just happens. You have to uh...well, you just have to at least make the effort to meet people." There was the silence again. She should drop it.

After a brief pause he said, "I meet people." She looked over at him.

"Yeah, I suppose you do," she said. "You meet people in the hospital, in the drug store, in the aisles of the grocery store. But what do you do? You say hello and goodbye and then you're on your way." She sighed. "When was the last time you had a date - I mean a real date - not lunch with friends?"

Rock was grinning. "Last year," he said.

"Really?" Liz was stunned.

"Yep, it was last year. I went out with Mary Jo Hilton."

"Who is Mary Jo Hilton?" Liz said looking a little annoyed.

"Don't you remember? Her billboards are everywhere." Rock knew Mary Jo enjoyed driving along the highways seeing her own face smiling down on the world. She would point to them with pride and an occasional smirk when they were together. "She and her father are joint partners in that commercial real estate office in Sparta. She asked me to lunch and I went out with her a few times after that."

"Well, you could have told me."

"You didn't ask," he said still grinning.

She smiled, realizing she was sounding petty and he was trying to get a rise out of her. "Well, fess up, tell me what happened?"

Rock shook his head. "She wasn't interested in a casual relationship, if you know what I mean. She wasn't subtle about it at all either. She kept talking about her biological clock and I could just tell she was anxious to get a ring on my finger, so I bowed out – and not too gracefully I'm afraid." As an afterthought he said, "Oh, and she never let me drive. I think she was ashamed of my truck."

Liz rolled her eyes and shook her head. "You're just an old rascal, Rock Clark," she said.

"I couldn't resist," he said. "I didn't share it with anyone at the time and you had your own worries. And anyway, that sounded a lot like a sermon you were preaching. You're not trying to marry me off like half the women in my congregation, are you? I've been introduced to so many sisters, daughters, and cousins twice-removed that I can't count them all," Rock said, smiling sideways at Liz.

"No, I don't guess I am," Liz said smiling back, "I would miss our conversations and I have a feeling if you had a wife, she would be jealous of our friendship."

"True." He looked at her with affection. "Some of my clergy friends say their wives are jealous of everything including their time spent working in the church, even though they know it goes with the territory."

The chair he sat in stopped rocking abruptly and he froze. Rock was looking at a place above her left shoulder. "Liz, don't move." he whispered. "Be ver-r-r-y still." He looked as if he'd seen a ghost.

"What!" she whispered back with alarm.

"There's a lizard on the back of your chair...shhh, don't move - he might jump on you."

She turned her head slightly to the left and found herself staring into the timid little eyes of a green anole. She gasped and tried to look startled. Then she turned in one swift motion and picked it up off the rocker. "Like this?" she asked and threw it in his direction. His rocker almost tipped over as he jumped out of it and ran off the porch.

"Hey!" he said. The lizard was terrified and ran over the side of the railing and into the azalea bushes. Liz was laughing hysterically. "That's just not funny at all," he said, but then he joined her back on the porch and they laughed until their sides hurt.

"Since when are you afraid of lizards?" she asked.

"Since one held me hostage in the 4th grade," he answered.

"I've got to hear this."

"You'll be scared too," he said and proceeded with the story.

As a child, he had spent two weeks each summer with his grandparents. Their dairy farm had two pastures for the cows. One pasture had a small creek running through it and the other had a fishing pond. After the grass was cropped clean in one, his grandfather would open the gate to the other so the cows could graze on fresh new grass, then close it again. After a morning of fishing in the pond, Rock started to open the gate to go into the next pasture which led back across the creek and to the house. A large lizard was sunning itself on the latch on the gate. Being a city boy, he had never encountered a lizard. He had read about the big lizards in South America that would attack a person. He was sure this was just a baby and its mother was somewhere close by just waiting for him to open the gate. He kept trying to get up nerve to shoo the lizard away, but the thought of the angry mother was too much for him. What seemed like hours later, his frantic grandmother – just knowing that he had drowned in the pond – came running up to the gate and rescued him.

"You poor baby, you must have been traumatized," Liz said with just a little sarcasm.

"You don't have a sympathetic bone in your body, Liz Logan," he said. "And you'd better watch your back; it's going to pay-back time for that lizard trick one of these days."

Another hour passed as they chatted. It was a quiet, comfortable and easy afternoon. When Rock prepared to leave, he picked up the empty tea pitcher and his glass to carry inside. "I'll get that," she said.

"That's okay, I'll carry it - you've got your hands full. You know Liz, your tea is intoxicating. Are you sure you don't spike it?"

Liz smiled and waved him off. "Get out of here, get back to work."

As she walked back in the house, she mumbled to herself. "I wish you found me half as intoxicating as you do my tea, Rock Clark." But then she mentally smacked herself for thinking such thoughts. Mary Jo Hilton, was it? She recalled now seeing Mary Jo's smiling face on real estate billboards up and down the highway. Hmph!

She walked by the large antique mirror in the foyer. She pulled her hair up and studied her face. Her features were pleasant enough, she supposed. She had fine lines under her eyes and two creases in her forehead from squinting at the sun, but not so bad, she thought. She had good coloring and a natural rosy complexion so she wore only a sheer liquid foundation. Her hair was a warm brown, but recently she had noticed a few stray strands of gray mixed in with the brown. She ran her finger through her hair and yes, there they were; more than she remembered seeing before. And she could use a good cut too. The length made her face look too long and angular. She made a mental note to call her hairdresser in the morning. Or maybe she would make an appointment at that new place at the mall in Rock Hill. She had seen an ad in Friday's paper offering a total makeover with haircut and color for a discounted price. An updated look, that's what I need, she thought as she walked into the kitchen to put the tea pitcher in the dishwasher. She felt better just thinking about it. "Mary Jo Hilton - eat my dust," she murmured to no one in particular.

Rock sat at his desk and still couldn't get a handle on his sermon. Not only did he have Abigail on his mind, his conversation with Liz had made him think about Mary Jo. It was she who had kept initiating their dates. He met her at a charity dinner for the Children's Home and a few days later she invited him for an impromptu lunch at the Red Bowl. At first, he had been impressed with her intelligence. She had a master's degree in chemistry and fresh out of university had worked in research at a large chemical company in Atlanta. She had helped develop a new pesticide that was more environmentally friendly than what was on the market at the time. She had been recognized internationally and her research was published in several professional journals in her field.

Rock had asked her why she had given all that up and returned home to work in the real estate business with her father. Her answer was paltry at best. She said the real estate market was booming and her father needed her. She bragged that she could make more money in commercial real estate. "Money is what it's all about anyway, isn't it? You can say it isn't, Rock, but it all boils down to one thing – money does buy happiness." She had laughed as if daring him to disagree.

She always happened to have tickets to this and that – a concert in Charlotte, a theatre performance at the university. He turned down several invitations, but she kept calling him back. There was just no saying no to Mary Jo. Their conversations were always one-sided. It was plain and simple – Mary Jo was in love alright. But there was no way she could be in love with him; she hardly knew him because he never got a word in edgewise. Mary Joe was in love with Mary Jo and had this strange fixation on dating a preacher. She never introduced him as just Rock Clark – it was always The Reverend Rock Clark. It was embarrassing for heaven's sake. After several attempts to break things off, he got up the nerve to tell her that at this point in his life, he had no time for dating and he could not see her again. She was bitter, oh how she was bitter. No, he wouldn't be meeting anymore Mary Jo Hilton's, he thought.

"Unlucky in love," he said out loud. From Sandy Collins ditching him on prom night his senior year to Mary Jo Hilton and all the in betweens, it was enough to scare a man to death. Being a bachelor was beginning to sound more appealing every day. But there was still this little thread of hope that refused to go away.

He thought back to some of the couples he had counseled who were marrying again after one or both had lost a spouse. How do they get past their fears of losing a loved one again? He thought of Liz and Ron and how happy they had been together. Would Liz ever fall in love and marry again, he wondered. It gave him a start to realize that the image conjured up in his mind of Liz at the altar with another man bothered him immensely.

Enough pondering and back to my sermon - Pentecost Sunday. He thought through the seasons of the liturgical calendar: Christmas, Easter, Pentecost; Christmas was the birth of Christ, but just the birth of God's son would not save mankind. Only his death and resurrection could do that. But then came the birthday of the Christian Church - Pentecost - where God's spirit was blown in by a great wind descending upon everyone present - tongues of flame that descended from the Holy Spirit onto the disciples allowing them to have many gifts to heal and teach. What an earthshaking experience that must have been for the disciples, Rock thought. What if this happened today? He felt a gentle prodding in his heart as he always did as he prayed about his Sermon. "It is happening today, my child." God's voice as always soothed his soul. "It happens each time my spirit fills the heart of a new believer."

"Thank you, Lord," he said out loud. "There's my sermon."

***

The sermon seemed to revive him and his congregation. As they filed past, he could tell they had been moved by his words and he was humbled to think that God allowed him to be a vessel for His messages to the people. Bob Clayton's wife, Donna, told him it was a Sunday she would not soon forget. Even Edie Mosher had seemed interested and paid close attention to his sermon. He could see the frown on her face had softened, but all hopes that his words had somehow touched her disappeared when she refused to even come out the front door. He saw her driving out of the church parking lot without even looking his way.

Maura and Betty Anne Williams were the last ones out. As Rock had thought, Betty Anne had taken it upon herself to recruit some of the women to go by the hospital and sit with Holly now that she was out of intensive care. "What if she wakes up and no-one is in the room – she'll be scared half to death," she had told the ladies of the Presbyterian Women. It wasn't long before she had a full calendar and several had already sat by Holly's bedside. Maura had been on Friday and had called Rock afterwards. "Rock, I can't help but think about that poor girl all alone in the world. I look at her and think something like this could happen to one of my girls with no one to look after them. It makes me want to gather her close and tell her not to worry, we'll take care of her."

"You should meet the child," Rock had told her, and today she had. Rebecca brought Abby to church along with the regulars from Beverly Hills. She had sat as quiet as a mouse through the first part of the service taking everything in. When Rock finished the Children's Sermon and asked the little ones if they had any prayer requests, she raised her hand. She stood up and faced the congregation.

"Please pray for my mommy," she said with a solemn expression. "She's very sick." She sat back down and as Rock prayed, nearly every person in the church prayed in silence for Holly Spencer and her adorable little girl. The rustle of handkerchiefs being pulled from pockets and tissues being brought out of handbags was clearly audible.

Maura and Betty Anne met him as he was walking back up the steps. Maura shook his hand. "That was a wonderful service Rev Rock, and you were right - I think the whole church has fallen hard for little Abby. We'll treat her like our own grandchildren, won't we Betty Anne." Betty Anne nodded, "Don't you worry about it Rev Rock – that little one will have lots of grandma's in Park Place." Rock didn't doubt it one bit. He was always filled with wonder at the compassion that the women in the church always showed for others.

***

Monday morning was all a summer morning should

be. School had been out now for a week and she felt free as a bird. A golden glow on the horizon as the sun opened its sleepy eyes greeted Liz as she drove over the country roads to the hospital. Her mind wandered to all the beautiful sunrises she had seen in some of the places she had traveled. The Colorado Rockies and the coast of North and South Carolina are some of my favorite ones, she thought. A new dawn to a new day is something you never grow tired of. This morning was one of those extraordinary sunrises that make a person want to get out of bed early to see it every day of their life.

Then she thought about where she was headed - the hospital – the room where it was possible that Holly could be living out the final days of her life if her cancer was left untreated. The room on the West wing of the hospital where, even if she was aware of her surroundings, she still wouldn't be able to see a sunrise. But there were sunsets from that window, and they were equal in their beauty.

Liz wondered how it would feel to know that you had limited sunrises as Holly must have surely thought during her past cancer treatments. Now that time was healing the pain Liz had felt at Ron's sudden death of a heart attack, she thought it may be best to go suddenly – without a sense of dread of never seeing another sunrise. And in Holly's case, not knowing what would happen to her child when she was gone.

Liz was glad that Betty Ann had taken the initiative to recruit volunteers to spend hours at a time sitting at Holly's bedside. They were asked to read to her and talk to her even though she may not know they were there. It seemed somehow right that this young woman who had been so alone in her world, was now being surrounded by people who cared for her. They had filled the room with flowers and handmade quilts to make her surroundings pleasant in the hopes that they could somehow convey to Holly some love and warmth in her life. Park Place Presbyterian was filled with compassionate people and she had started thinking that maybe she should change her membership from the Methodist church. She had grown up in a Presbyterian church but Ron had been brought up as a Methodist and she had let him make the decision on denominations after they had married.

How would I handle it if I knew my days were so limited, she thought, as many scenarios went through her mind, knowing that none of us are guaranteed another sunrise. Liz felt that Holly's sunrises would not be over if she lost her battle with cancer. Whatever mission she had been on when she left her hometown took courage, determination and faith. The worn Bible found in her car was full of highlighted scripture verses about faith and salvation. Jess had retrieved it from the car that night and had put it in her hospital room. It was a comfort to all who visited her as they thumbed through it and recognized some of the verses she had highlighted. So, no, Holly's sunrises would not disappear with her last breath. They'll just be beginning – taking her to the place where sunrises begin and with the One who makes them - the place where Ron was now residing. As she turned into the hospital parking lot, she said a quick prayer thanking God for her own faith and salvation which would lead her to that same place someday.

CHAPTER 13

Rock pulled into the parking lot of the post office and was glad to see no other cars. He needed stamps and didn't have time to wait in line. He was already pushing it to get the monthly newsletters out before Betty closed at 5 p.m. Where did the month of May go? It was already the first week of June! He carried the newsletters in so he could put stamps on them at the side counter. Up until six months ago it was rare to see over two or three people inside the post office at the same time but the completion of the first phase of the Sun's Up Retirement Village on the edge of town had changed all that. Everyone agreed that it had somewhat changed the dynamics of the place. It was losing its small community post office appeal, but it did pump up the revenue needed to keep it open when so many small towns were losing their post offices due to the financial condition of the US Postal Service.

"I've got a package for you Rev Rock." Betty scanned the tracking code on the package. "And what a lofty title for a country parson!" she said as she handed the package to him.

"What title is that?" he asked.

The Most Reverend Rockford W. Clark" – that's what this package says anyway."

"Hmm...The Most Reverend – they must be trying to butter me up for the kill," he said opening the large envelope. It was a catalog from an online seminary. "Aha!

'Get your doctor of divinity degree in just six months with our easy internet course'. By golly, I think I'll do it!" They both laughed.

"Well you are the Most Reverend Rockford Clark we have in Park Place because you're the only Reverend Rockford Clark we got. Now there!" Betty batted her big brown eyes and looked at him with a pouty stare. "And what's this with you sneaking in the post office checking your box without coming in to say hello? You did that yesterday, you know." Rock knew that one was coming. Betty always scolded him if he didn't come in to speak to her – but sometimes he was in a hurry.

"You had a big crowd – I didn't want to bother you. Besides you were in animated conversation with that Superman looking railroad construction worker who's been coming in all week and I knew you wouldn't give me the time of day." Aha, I got you back, he thought. But it was near impossible to get one over on Betty.

"Hmph! Well, you could'a just stuck your head in the door and spoke. Just 'cause I'm flirting with Superman don't mean I don't have time to speak – unlike some people I know."

"I'll do better," Rock said laying his newsletters on the counter. "I do miss your sweet face and sassy mouth and it's been awhile since I've heard any good gossip." He handed her the church credit card.

"You want a hundred stamps, I suppose." She ran the card through and handed him the stamps. "Hand me some of those mailers and I'll help you put stamps on 'em. It'll take you all day and I close in thirty minutes. You got a bad habit of comin' in here right at closing time."

As they peeled the stamps off and put them on the envelopes, Betty broke the silence. "Speaking of gossip, Rev Rock, you're fast becoming the hot topic." She glanced at him for his reaction.

"Well, if it has to be someone, it may as well be me," he said.

"Don't you even want to know what they're saying?" She stopped and leaned over the counter waiting for him to acknowledge her.

"Well, I know you're going to tell me anyway, so let's have it."

With a satisfactory smirk, she leaned back. "It's you and Miss Liz that's causing all the buzz," she said.

"Me? Liz? Whatever for?" he asked innocently.

"Because you're always sittin' on her porch drinkin' tea, that's what for!"

"That's because her porch used to be my porch and besides I don't have a big enough porch to drink tea on," he said. Rock always came out of the post office feeling better than he did going in. Gossip? Wait 'til I tell Liz about this.

CHAPTER 14

"People are going to start talking," Rock said when he came out on the porch with a glass of tea. Liz was already in her rocker with hers.

"They already are," said Liz with a grin. Rock looked surprised. He thought Betty had just been teasing him.

"Really? What are they saying." She laughed and kept rocking. He put his glass on the porch rail and sat down in the chair beside her. He scooted the chair around so he could face her. She had turned off the porch light so as not to attract the flying moths and mosquitoes. The streetlight glowed through the rose covered lattice and caught Rock's puzzled expression.

"The thing is, I just feel more at home on this old porch than I do on mine. I spent so much time out here over the years jotting down my thoughts for my sermons. I just think better out here." The windows were open and Liz noticed that a gentle breeze was billowing the sheer fabric of the curtains in and out of the window. She loved this old porch too.

"You know you're welcome here anytime you want to come by - whether I'm here or not," said Liz. "Besides, a little gossip gives them something to do. It doesn't bother me." He relaxed and again, they settled comfortably in the porch rockers, with the familiar squeaking and creaking as they rocked. The noise intermingled with the other sounds of the night, the cicadas and tree frogs and the bark of Irma Rembert's dog.

"This is nice," he said, and wondered again if it was just the porch that gave him that warm glow or if it was the company he was keeping. "Remind me to shoot some WD-40 on that rocker," he said, as he had a dozen times before.

"I wish you would shoot some WD-40 on Irma's crazy barking dog," Liz said with a laugh.

"Just find me a can – I'll see what I can do."

"You wouldn't get near that dog," she said.

"Well, if he bites as much as he barks, you wouldn't either!" He enjoyed their easy banter, but when Liz looked up at him, it was with a more serious expression.

"Rock, when is your appointment with Dr. Braem and the oncologist?"

"It's Wednesday afternoon and I've been thinking about taking Abby by to see Holly this week. I promised her over a week ago I would take her and I'm ashamed to say that I've been avoiding it. I'm just afraid she'll panic when her mother doesn't wake up.

Liz looked up. "She's such a precocious little thing. She's started calling me Miss Whiz. Her vocabulary is amazing and her pronunciation is exceptional and she's not having one bit of trouble saying her L's any other time. I think she's just trying to get a rise out of me. I corrected her today, but she just kept right on calling me Miss Whiz, looking at me with that sweet little innocent face."

"Miss Whiz, is it? I like that." She could see the mischief in his eyes

"I thought you would find that amusing," she said and threw an ice cube at him. "Seriously though, I don't think it would do any harm to take her to see Holly. I think it would assure her and make her feel less frightened. What do you think?"

Liz watched him as he ran his fingers through his hair and propped his feet up on the porch railing. I wonder if he knows how I feel about him, she thought. Of course not, I don't even know how I feel about him.

"Holly does still have a feeding tube and an IV in but at least she's not hooked up to all the other tubes and monitors like she was in the beginning. I don't think Abigail would notice that much. The bruising on her face is fading too. I think it might even be good for Holly. Hearing Abby's voice would be therapeutic. As Peter said, you never know what they can hear. I'll talk to him about it."

Liz yawned. "Okay," she said. Rock looked at his watch and was surprised to see it was after 10.

"Oh man! You need to get to bed, I didn't mean to hold you up - you've got an early appointment. Give me a call when you get back in tomorrow and we'll arrange the visit."

"These longer days do make me forget about the time," Liz said as she and Rock stood up at the same time.

"Thanks, Liz." Rock gave her a sheepish grin. "I rock on your porch, I drink your tea and then I disappear into the night." They both laughed.

Liz watched him as he stepped off the porch and into the night. She touched the back of the chair he had sat in as she walked past it into the house. She closed the windows and thought about Ron as she walked back to their empty bedroom. "Ron," she whispered. "I wish you were still here and I wouldn't be going through this. I loved you so much. Are these crazy feelings I have for Rock just loneliness?" She wished he was there to answer – but for some reason, she didn't feel the heartache and loneliness that she usually felt when she thought of Ron. She turned the sheets back and then went into the tiny bathroom to wash her face and brush her teeth. She brushed back her hair. She liked the new cut and she didn't look quite so washed out with the soft color the hairdresser had added. Rock hadn't even noticed. So much for that!

***

Rock walked across the old brick pathway that led to the church courtyard. He then followed a similar, but new brick pathway to his house. They had tried to match the early 20th century brick but couldn't get it quite right. Maybe after a few years, it would look more natural. He looked back at the house he had once called home and was glad that Liz lived there instead of someone who would not welcome his frequent visits. Rats! He had intended to tell her that she looked nice tonight. She had done something different with her hair. "Miss Whiz," he said out loud and all of a sudden, he had a spring in his step and a song in his heart as he opened the door of the big lonely house he now called home.

CHAPTER 15

I am confident of this, that the one who began a good work
among you will bring it to completion by the day of Jesus
Christ.

~ Philippians 1:6

Peter Braem had set up the meeting with Dr. Lesley
Woods, an oncologist from Charlotte. She was to meet
with them in Peter's office in the hospital at 4:15 after
she had gone over Holly's medical records and done a
complete evaluation of her recent scans. Rock arrived at
3:55 and sat in one of the waiting rooms. A discarded
newspaper was in the chair beside him and he skimmed
through it to kill time. There were rumors that a water
park was being built just across the river in the
neighboring county. The newspaper promised to be the
first to report it when and if it was true. He had just
started reading the comics when Peter Braem walked in
and motioned him to his office.

There was an additional chair pulled up and Rock sat
in it. "It's going to be up to you to make the final
decisions Rock," Pete told him. Dr. Woods and I will
discuss the treatment options and tell you what we think
is best, but we can't make the call. You now have legal
authority to choose her path of treatment since she's not
in any condition to choose for herself."

"But she's already made that choice, hasn't she?"
Rock was torn; Holly had made her decision in Ohio not

to seek further treatment. "How can I go against her wishes?"

"You'll know," said Peter. "Dr. Woods is also a Christian - that's why I chose her. We're going to need some divine guidance here."

Dr. Lesley Woods was an attractive redhead - not at all what Rock had been expecting. She was vivacious and friendly but got right down to business as soon as introductions had been made. She didn't waste time on formalities and called him by his first name just as she did with Dr. Braem. She addressed each of them. "Pete - Rock," she looked at them individually and continued. "From everything I see, I feel good about starting an aggressive method of treatment on Holly right away. There's been very little change since her scans in Columbus. The cancer in the kidney seems to be contained and hasn't spread...yet." She paused. "I don't think we can afford to wait much longer." Peter looked at Rock and started to say something, but Dr. Woods continued. "I concur with Dr. Wang in Ohio that removing that kidney and starting radiation on the tumor on the frontal lobe of the brain will give her very good odds for survival. She's young and it bothers me a lot that she had made the decision to decline treatment." She looked at Peter and then back to Rock. "Pete and I have talked and we agree that her ability to make sound decisions could have been impaired by the location of the tumor. Dr. Wang in Columbus agrees."

Rock thought for a moment. It was not in his character to go against a dying person's wishes but there was more at stake here. Abby's life would be forever affected by the decision he made now. He had prayed for days about this and he knew what he had to do and spoke up. "I don't know what God's plans are for Holly, but somehow I don't think He would want to take a mother away from her child. Maybe he used this accident - as horrible as it is - to take the decision making away from her and put it upon someone who can think rationally. I'll sign whatever paperwork necessary to start her treatments." Both doctors nodded in approval. They joined hands and Rock led them in prayer. Dr. Woods turned to Peter. "How soon can you release her to be transferred to Charlotte for surgery? It will be at least a week before I can work it into my schedule."

Peter smiled. "You schedule the operating room and we'll have her there."

Dr. Woods sat back down. "In the meanwhile, we'll start radiation on that tumor. Your people here at the hospital can handle that, can't they?" Rock felt a fresh air of optimism in the room.

"Pete, one more thing - I'll leave while you and Dr. Woods handle the details, but I've made plans to bring the little girl by to see Holly this afternoon. I hope that's alright."

Pete walked over to Rock as he stood at the door and shook his hand. "Rock, I know this is tough on you having to rely on our information to make these decisions about Miss Spencer's care. I think it's a perfect time for the child to see her mother now before we start radiation treatments. Thank you for all you've done."

Rock walked out of Peter's office feeling lighter than when he walked in. Seeking God's guidance had made the decision-making much easier. He walked down the hallway and stopped at room 114. The young woman lying in the bed looked as if she was just sleeping. He sat down beside her and held her hand. "I wonder how many burdens you've carried on your shoulders young lady," he said. "Many more than a woman your age should have to bear, I'm sure. Holly, I've made a decision for you today that I felt was right. I pray to God that you will agree it was the right one when this is all over." He squeezed her hand. He knew it was next to impossible, but he could almost feel her squeezing back. He sat there for a minute and just watched her. He felt a connection with her - he could almost picture Jan in her place - his sweet Jan, whose hopes and dreams were never fulfilled. Losing her had crushed his spirit for much too long and he didn't want the same thing to happen to Abby. He spoke once more, but this time to God.

"Lord, Jan died much too young and I had no choice in the matter, even though I begged and longed for her to live. You have given Holly another chance. I pray that someday she will be grateful for it. But may your will be done. Amen." He turned around and started out of the room just in time to see Liz walking past the nurse's station holding Abby by the hand.

When Abby spotted Rock, she broke loose from Liz and came running to meet him, almost knocking him over as she sprang into his arms. "Is my mommy in there?" She could barely contain her excitement. Rock opened the door a little wider. Liz had caught up to them - it warmed her heart to see Abby's excitement as she ran to her mother's bedside - and it warmed her heart even more when she saw the look of tenderness and compassion on Rock's face as he watched the two of them. He would have made a wonderful father, she thought.

"Mommy, Mommy – I've missed you so much!"

Liz had told her beforehand that mommy was sleeping and she could talk all she wanted to Holly, but Holly couldn't talk back just yet. "Yes, I know," she had said, "she's still healing." She couldn't believe how much she seemed to understand. "She's been sick before," Abby said as if that explained everything.

It was no trouble at all for Abby to carry on a one-way conversation with her mother. She told her about Miss Rebecca and all the children; about all the good food Miss Estelle was cooking and about going to Sunday School. She told her that Bernie missed her too and that Miss Rebecca was going to wash Bernie in the laundry and next time she came to visit he could come too. "He has too many germs right now," she said, "and I know you don't like germs."

Rock and Liz laughed and were amazed that Abby was taking it all in stride. After she had talked herself out, she asked Rock if she could lay down beside her mother. Liz walked out in the hall to ask if it was okay. Jamie Webster walked back to the room with her.

"Of course, you can lay down with your mommy, Miss Abigail," she said with a big grin.

Abby grinned back. "How did you know my name?"

"Well, that's easy enough. You've got a big sign on your back that says, "Abigail Spencer – Hug me." Abby swirled around and then laughed.

"You're just teasing me, aren't you?"

"Yes Ma'am, I am, but I'm not teasing you about cuddling up with Mommy. Here, let me help you up." She reached down to pick up the little girl who was as light as a feather and sat her gingerly down beside Holly. Abby moved closer to her mother and touched her hand where the IV was inserted.

"Does that hurt?" she asked Jamie.

"No, Abby, it doesn't hurt, but be careful that you don't pull it out."

"I'll be very careful," she said and reached out and touched her mother on the cheek. She cupped Holly's face in both little hands. "I'll take care of you when we get home Mommy. Hurry up and get well." She leaned over and kissed her on the cheek and then scooted a little closer and laid her head in the crook of her mother's arm.

Liz sniffled and picked up a tissue to wipe away a few tears.

"Where's mine?" said Rock, and she handed him one too.

"Don't leave me out," said Jamie as she took one from the box and blew her nose.

"Thank you for breaking the rules a little Jamie" – he knew she had.

Jamie winked at them.

I didn't break 'em – just bent 'em a little," she said as she walked out the door and started to close it. She glanced back and saw that Rock and Liz were already in deep conversation. Hmm, she thought to herself, there may be something to the gossip after all - the Presbyterian preacher and the high school guidance counselor. She couldn't resist. She stuck her head back in the door. "Rev

Rock?" Rock looked up surprised to find her still there.

"Yes, Jamie?"

"I think you took my advice and started beating on some doors."

Rock looked puzzled for a second but then his face registered that he got her meaning. He blushed but put up a good front.

"You never know what you'll find in your own backyard," he said and winked back at her. She laughed and did her little happy dance and she walked out the room and closed the door. Liz looked at Rock.

"What was that all about?"

Rock smiled. "Jamie - just being Jamie."

Liz turned around. "Look at that," she said. Abby was sound asleep snuggled up against her mother. At just that moment, Maura walked in the door and took in the scene.

"Where are the tissues?" she asked. Liz handed her the box. Maura volunteered to stay in the room while Liz and Rock went to get a bite to eat.

"You drive," said Liz.

"You don't mind riding in my beat-up old truck?" Rock said with surprise.

"I've ridden in plenty of old pickup trucks," she said. "I was raised on a farm, you know. Anyway, your truck isn't beat up - just well used."

He opened the passenger door and she got in. "Where to?" he asked.

"Let's go to the new bistro on Catawba Avenue."

"The Bistro it is," he said and the motor sprung to life.

***

Betty was waiting for him when he walked into the post office the next morning. She started the conversation as if they had just left off from a few days before. "Aha - I told you so."

"You're always telling me so Betty. I can't keep up with everything you tell me - what is it this time?"

"You think if you go to these little hidden-away eating places, no one will see you?"

"Betty, Betty - if I didn't want anyone to see me I would become a hermit."

"You know what I'm talking about - traipsing off down Catawba Avenue with a certain guidance counselor."

"Why Betty, I think you're just jealous!"

"Hmph! You're just puffed up like a' old peacock if you think I'm jealous. Besides, you're not my type," she said grinning from ear to ear. "I go for the bad boys myself."

CHAPTER 16

*T*he second is this: 'Love your neighbor as yourself.' There
is no commandment greater than these."

~ Mark 12:31 NIV

Monday morning at the Feed & Seed found the
friends sitting on their respective bags of feed in Junie's
store. Junie made a point of pointing out the Ol' Roy bag.
"There, I hope you're happy," he said to Fred.

Rock had just finished with a prayer of praise for
Kathleen's test results. "It's not her heart after all," Junie
had told them. "It's just an infection around the heart -
Perio - something."

"Pericarditis," Rock said. He knew that Pericarditis
often caused chest pain and sometimes other symptoms
that mimic more serious heart problems.

"Yeah, that's it! She's on some medication to clear it
up and she's already up and cooking again. Thank the
Lord - I was dang near about to starve to death."

"Junie, don't be telling tall tales," Larry guffawed. "As
much as you like to eat, you're not going to starve to
death!"

Junie grinned. "Well, to tell you the truth, those
ladies over at Kathleen's church brought enough food in
to feed half the county. I've never seen the like - I even
took food over to Cap's a time or two just to get rid of it."

Cap Price had been a regular at the Feed & Seed for

many years, buying seed, plants and fertilizer. Age and Josie's illness had slowed his farming down considerably. He still sold a few vegetables during the summer months, but he was only able to farm a small portion of what he once had. Since Josie's death, he had started coming back into the Feed and Seed – more for company than anything else. Recently he had begun to come in while the guys were having their Monday morning meeting and stand in the background just listening. They would try to pull him into the conversation but he never said much.

Junie confided that he was worried about Cap. "He's not acting right," he said. "It's not like Cap to be so quiet."

"I think he's depressed," said Larry. Rock looked at Larry.

"You may be right."

"Yeah, my sister suffers from depression," said Fred. "That's what it is."

"Depression – hmm, I never would have thought of that," said Junie. "I've heard there's some pills you can take to cure it. Maybe we ought'a take him to the doctor." Rock watched his friends with amusement. The Monday Morning Bunch - between the four of us, he thought, we could solve every problem in Park Place.

Junie went on - "I know he's not eating right. He comes in here just about every day. I give him a pack of nabs and a Ne-Hi when he's here at lunch and God only knows what he eats for dinner – and I swear to you Rev Rock – I know he don't eat breakfast, the way he wolfs down those nabs. Kathleen will come in sometimes with a bacon and egg biscuit and give it to him. She'll tell him he might as well eat it since my 'glycerides are up and I'm not allowed to have but one. Now she's started puttin' a banana in the bag with the biscuit."

Rock was touched by their generosity. "You and Kathleen have a big heart," he said. "It's a good thing you're doing."

"Anybody would do the same if they just knew it," said Junie, but Rock knew that wasn't true. Most people wouldn't take the time to notice.

Rock wasn't sure if it was depression or if it was a financial thing. Cap lived in a modest little house on Chance Cove. He thought about going to visit him but remembered he was a member of the Methodist Church.

"I think I'll go talk to Bob Hartley at the Methodist Church. Maybe he can get to the bottom of it."

***

Bob was on the phone when Rock walked into his office. The Methodist Church had been built at around the same time as Park Place Presbyterian and had basically the same layout. The office was almost identical to the way his office had been before they remodeled and moved it out to the carriage house. It was in the original church building and was located right behind the choir loft in a small crowded room. There were two desks, but Rock wondered how Bob and the church secretary ever fit in there at the same time. It would have made him claustrophobic. There was a small restroom and coat closet on one side of the room and a well-worn leather sofa and chair on the other. The rest of the wall space was lined with bookcases and file cabinets. The desks were right in the center. The secretary's desk was unoccupied at the time and Bob motioned for Rock to have a seat in her chair. Rock noticed the crutches leaning against the wall behind Bob's chair. "How's that leg?" he asked.

"Painful," he answered. "It's not mending like they thought it would. The Bishop wants me to take some sick leave and pull in a replacement and I'm beginning to think he is a wise old man."

"I don't think it's a financial thing Rock," Bob said as Rock told him his concerns about Cap. "The last time I discussed it with him, he told me that he and Josie had put a little money aside - not a whole lot, but enough that he doesn't need any assistance from the church. But his grief is strong and I wouldn't rule out depression. Sometimes when an older person loses a spouse, they don't have any desire to cook or eat at home - maybe that's why he eats so much when he's out and about. Rock hadn't thought about that.

"I feel so helpless not being able to get out and visit him!" Rock could see the frustration in the eyes of his colleague and friend and he knew what he should do, but how was he going to fit yet another thing in his already busy schedule. This is what I get for being a busybody, he thought.

"Bob, if you don't mind, I can go out and visit him." The words just came out of his mouth and relief flooded his good friend's face.

"Would you do that for me, Rock? I'm so grateful that you offered." Rock knew his plate was already full and he'd been trying to work in visits to his own flock, but what could he do? With a guilty conscience, he thought about Edie Mosher for a moment, he still hadn't been out to visit her. He felt the same old sense of dread, but pushed it to the back of his mind. He would go see Cap - Bob would do the same for him if the tables were turned. Bob seemed to know what he was thinking.

"You're an answer to prayer Rock," he said with feeling. "The good Lord always helps us find a way – even when we doubt that we can do what needs to be done. He's given you a special gift Rock – the ability to discern where there's a real need and the compassion to do something about it. Don't ever take that gift lightly."

He was humbled by his friend's words and walked out knowing that somehow he could work it all out, even with Edie.

"Lord, forgive me for doubting," he said in a small whispered prayer.

***

Chance Cove was a dead-end road that came to an abrupt halt at a small boat ramp built by the families on the road to access the river. All sorts of wildlife could be found here – the Great Blue Heron had nesting sites all up and down the river, but they seemed to favor Chance Cove. Deer trails were abundant and it wasn't unusual to see dozens grazing in the soybean fields that ran parallel with the unpaved road.

There were only four houses on the road - modest clapboard houses that had been built during the 1940's - most of them still occupied by descendants of the same families who had built them. James Burnett and Hilda Grant's parents had lived side by side on the road. James and Hilda had grown up as sweethearts, had married and after both sets of parents died, inherited both houses. They had moved into the Grant house when Hilda's parents had passed away and their only daughter and her husband now lived in the Burnett house with their two children.

Madge Johnson's house had stood empty since the day she entered the Presbyterian Home in Florence. It was now being rented to some family friends until it sold. Madge was one of Rock's favorite people – he had eaten many a meal in the little white house with purple shutters. She dressed as flamboyantly as she painted her shutters – always wearing bright and bold colors. Rock had driven down to Florence in April to visit both Madge and Cecil Alexander, another member of Park Place Presbyterian. Madge had left her card game and rushed to greet him with a smile and a big kiss to the left of his nose. As he passed the large mirror in the lobby, he noticed that her signature bright red lipstick had left its mark and he was amused when he saw that half a dozen other gentlemen in the room wore the same mark on the same cheek. There were a lot of bedazzled men at the Presbyterian Home when Madge was in the room. Madge had told him she would soon be putting her house on the market to sell. Her son was adamant that she not live by herself. "And Rev Rock, don't you say a word, but that daughter-in-law of mine would drive me crazy if I had to live with them. No, I'll just sell my house so I can live in comfort here with all my friends." She smiled and waved at Dexter, the man in the blue shirt, as he waited with growing impatience for her to get back to the card table.

Rock drove by the house and noticed that the front lawn was still well maintained and Madge's daylilies were blooming profusely. He thought it must be hard to leave a home where so many fond memories had been made, but Madge had seemed happy enough with her decision.

Cap's was the last house on the winding road and had a splendid view of the river. He and Josie had bought it cheap when they married in the mid-fifties. The house had always seemed small with just two bedrooms, a kitchen, living room and one bath but Cap had confided to the friends at the Feed and Seed that now that Josie was gone, it seemed much too big for his liking.

Rock had to stop for a white car to back out of the driveway before he pulled in. A white Mercedes - hmm – could it be? Sure enough, a Rampage Realty decal covered the passenger side door and as the car pulled around facing him, even with the huge designer sunglasses, he knew who it was. He waved but Mary Jo didn't acknowledge that she saw him. She hit the gas pedal and spun gravel as she pulled away. "Now what's with that?" he said out loud. They had not parted on the best of terms, but she had no reason to speed away and snub him. He pulled on in and opened the door. It was a good five degrees cooler here underneath the shade trees that led down to the riverbank.

Cap was sitting in a weathered rocking chair on the porch laughing when Rock walked up the steps. "I thought that real estate lady was gonna blow you off the road," he said. Rock laughed at him.

"I tried to read the sign on her car door. I think it said, 'eat my dust'." Cap's grin deepened.

"What I told her didn't make her none too happy. I suppose she was trying to dust me up a mite."

"I figured she was lost back here off the beaten path," Rock said.

"Nope." Cap's face was more serious now. "Not yet anyway but I suggested that she start working on it. She was trying to badger me and wouldn't take no for an answer. I told her to get lost." Rock was surprised at the irritation in the older man's voice. He was usually so mild mannered and ever so polite to women. At least he wasn't showing any signs of depression now. He seemed downright feisty.

"Well, are you going to tell me what she was badgering you about or am I going to have to make three guesses?"

"Pull up a chair," said Cap, pointing to the smaller matching rocker that had belonged to Josie.

Rock was seething when he backed out of Cap's driveway. Cap had told him that Mary Jo had approached all the property owners on Chance Cove trying to buy them out for a little more than market value and was very pushy about it. She had met opposition from all but Madge's son who no longer had ties to the land now that Madge was in Florence. She said she wanted to build a condominium community but Rock felt there was more to it than that.

"I could use the money," Cap had told him. "I'm land rich and cash poor, but I'll be doggoned if I'm going to sit back and watch all this pretty land messed up with those ugly old buildings. I'm going to see if James and Hilda's daughter will take me over to Clinton to see Madge Johnson. She'll straighten out that son of hers."

This might be just the thing for Cap, he thought. He's got something worth fighting for. He wondered again if he should get caught up in the middle of this – something that was none of his business. Then he remembered Bob's words. Besides, he hated to see someone take advantage of the elderly in the community. He would go down to the courthouse tomorrow and see if there was a change in zoning to allow for multiple housing units.

"Watch out Mary Jo," he said as he pulled back on the main highway. "You picked a fight with the wrong old man." Cap Price had dug in with both heels.

CHAPTER 17

Rock had to push Theo off the table twice while he was eating breakfast. "Okay, big boy. Since you're not going to let me eat in peace, I'll lock you back up in the laundry room until you finish your breakfast and I finish mine." Theo gave him an ugly look and took off like a flash. He pulled out his calendar as he finished breakfast and decided he just might have time to squeeze in a haircut before he went by the zoning office.

"You're going five miles for a haircut when Luther Riggins is right here in town!" Reva was admonishing Rock for what she perceived to be his "lack of gumption." "You're just a big ol' chicken, that's what you are."

"Chicken!" Wouldn't you be worried if someone who was mad at you gave you a haircut? I was going to start going to Fred anyway."

"Luther ain't mad at you – he's just grumpy. He's like that with everybody now and again. What did you do to him anyway?"

"Me? I didn't do anything to Luther - I just asked him when he was going on vacation and he said he didn't have time to go on vacation and stomped off. What did I say wrong?"

"Maybe he's grumpy because he hasn't been on vacation. Maybe he can't afford to go on vacation and here you are taking money out of his pocket to get a haircut at Fred's."

He couldn't win with Reva – she was always one up

on him. "Well, I'm not about to let someone in a bad mood get a hold of my hair. He'll probably give me a buzz cut just for spite."

"Well, it wouldn't hurt you any if he did cut it short. You're beginning to look like one of those hippies from back in the sixties." Rock walked out before her exaggerations got out of hand. If she got wound up, she would be comparing his hair to the dark-skinned Jesus in the frame hanging behind her desk.

He did have plenty of hair he thought as he adjusted his visor mirror to give his hair a quick comb through. His thick head of dark hair was one of his small vanities. He was not superstitious but he always felt a little guilty that he might be overly proud of it and somehow end up going bald. And Reva was halfway right at least – it was sticking out over his ears. He stopped thinking about it and enjoyed the pleasant drive out the winding country road to Fred's little backyard barber shop.

When Rock arrived, he had to wait in line for Bo Evans and his grandson. Bo's wife Dorothy had come in to make sure the men didn't conspire to cut off Little Bo's curls. Dorothy was a talker and Rock had been looking forward to a little peace and quiet, but she motioned him to the seat next to her when he walked in the door. "Why Rev Rock, what are you doing way out here? Is Luther on the rampage again?"

This was the last conversation he wanted to get into. Changing the subject, he replied to Dorothy, "We missed you two at church Sunday - how was your trip to the mountains?"

"Lord have mercy, Rev Rock, don't ever go to the

mountains with Bo Evans" she said. "Bo barreled through Cherokee so fast, I know there wasn't a feather left on any of those Indians' heads. I wanted to stop at some of those roadside stands and get Little Bo a black bear or some little moccasins, but no-o-o. Bo was in such an all fired hurry to get to Bryson City, he didn't even slow down. It was always 'hurry up and get there – hurry up and get there' and when we got there it was 'hurry up and get home'. No siree, Rev Rock, don't ever go to the mountains with Bo Evans." Rock didn't plan to – he had heard enough stories about Bo's race car days on the local dirt track.

Little Bo's haircut was finished and Fred started on Bo's. Dorothy walked outside with her grandson and Rock settled back with a Field & Stream Magazine.

"Why don't you let me get rid of this comb-over Bo – it looks ridiculous," Fred said as he put a black plastic cape around Bo's neck.

Alarmed, Bo reached up and put his hand flat on his head, "Don't you touch my comb-over, Fred - I'd rather have it look ridiculous than to have no hair at all." "Besides, I've got a pointy head."

Fred combed through his hair "You do have a pointy head – well, at least let me change the part a little. This one's all the way down to your ear."

"Go ahead," Bo sighed, "If it'll make you happy. I should'a just gone to see Luther if I'd wanted to be scalped again. He's still mad at me for leaving a $2 tip. I thought $2 was just about right, what do you think Fred?"

"I would think I'd died and gone to heaven if I got a $2 tip. People don't tip much out here in the boondocks."

Rock smiled as he was reading his magazine – the chitchat between two good friends was a relaxing sound in little country barber shops. The next thing Rock knew, Fred's yell of "NEXT" jerked him out of a pleasant doze and he walked out 20 minutes later with a decent looking haircut and made sure he left a crisp $5 bill on Luther's counter. Everybody needs to feel a touch of heaven now and then, he thought.

Reva had a sandwich waiting for him when he got back to the office. "You've just got time to eat. The Kramers are coming in to talk to you about joining the church. Mr. Kramer said you had called him last week and invited them to come by. He couldn't believe you called so quickly after they left a visitor card in the collection plate. He said he'd been to four churches since they moved here and not yet had a call from the preacher." Rock was glad they were coming - they seemed like a nice couple and had visited several Sundays in a row.

"That's because you go through the cards every week and put them on my desk. I can't help but be efficient when I've got such a good secretary." Reva's face beamed. With these appointments, he knew he wouldn't have time to go by the zoning office today. "Thanks for making the appointment Reva. Will you mark a 9 o'clock meeting on my calendar for tomorrow morning?"

"Sure thing."

He got a bottle of water out of the refrigerator and opened his sandwich. "I don't know how you do it," he said. Reva looked up at him questioningly. "Roast Beef, green peppers and Swiss cheese - you can read my mind, dear lady. That's my most favorite sandwich ever."

Reva smiled. "I'm not reading your mind - just reading the refrigerator. That's all that was in there."

"I suppose I need to make a grocery store run. I'd rather have a tooth pulled."

"Somebody sure needs to or you're going to starve to death and you won't need any teeth pulled. By the way, if you see Miss Liz tonight, take these dishes back to her. She was sweet as could be and brought lunch to me one day last week. That's one fine lady in case you hadn't noticed, hint, hint." Rock pretended he didn't hear her.

Rock used the excuse of dropping the dishes off when he walked over to the cottage. He looked up from the tray Liz had put on the side table between the two of them. It was filled with tiny sandwiches, cheese straws and a small bowl of handmade mints. There was a pitcher of some kind of pink punch - leftovers, she had said - from the Park Place Woman's Club the night before. He didn't know how many he should eat. The whole plate of the tiny things didn't look much larger than a big sandwich. He decided he would take two and watch to see what Liz would do. "Have you been back to see Abby since her hospital visit?"

"I went by there today," said Liz, munching on a cheese straw. "Rebecca says she was on cloud nine when I returned her from her visit with Holly. She told all the other kids about it and held them captive with her description of the hospital room and the nurses but she still cries for her mommy every night – daytime, she's fine, but when it's time to tuck her in at night, she cries. She said nobody can read her a book like her mommy and that her mommy sings her some special song before she goes to bed at night. She sang a few lines to Rebecca. It was in a foreign language. Rebecca said she lost her on the first stanza."

They sat there in silence for a few minutes. Rock watched Liz as she poured him another glass of punch. She pushed the sandwiches to his side of the table between them and he picked up another one. She reached over and pinched a few of the spent flowers from the rose bush behind him. He breathed in deeply as he smelled the fresh fragrance that she was wearing - camellia blossoms, he thought - that's what she smells like. He decided then and there that he loved the smell of camellias. He had a sudden urge to reach over and hold her hand, but stopped himself before he could act on his strange compulsion. Rock Clark, he admonished himself. Whatever has gotten into you... She turned around and caught him staring at her and looked puzzled.

He was embarrassed and changed the subject. "I went by the hospital today. They've already started radiation on Holly."

She sighed. That wasn't what she had hoped he would say.

CHAPTER 18

The zoning department was utilizing space in the basement of Carter's Drug Store on the corner of Main and Third while the new county government building was being built. It had its own entrance from the street level by just walking down a flight of concrete steps.

"Threw us out, they did – lock, stock and barrel," said Marty McAteer as he got down the zoning ordinance book. "The inspections department has doubled in size since the Sun's Up Retirement Village came in. I sure hope they hurry with our new building – this damp old basement is taking a toll on all our records."

"I imagine so," said Rock.

"Of course, they're talking about going digital with all these records anyway," piped in Polly Gamble.

"Won't be the same," said Marty. "I think that'll be the day I retire."

Polly nodded, "Me too."

Rock walked up to the counter where Marty had opened the book. "Now what would they do without you two? Between the two of you, you know the whole county's zoning ordinances by heart."

"If they don't quit changing 'em at the drop of a hat, I won't know squat," Marty said with more than a little exasperation in his tone. "Every time somebody comes in that might make a few dollars revenue for the county, the old zones just go out the window."

Rock was curious. "They have to inform the community, don't they?"

"Well, they put up zoning signs, but the signs are so small and they get lost amongst all the real estate signs so that nobody much notices 'em anymore. You would be surprised at how few people show up at these zoning meetings and then they come in here later complaining about industrial stuff going up right alongside their houses. Why, just a couple of months ago, this big theme park company applied for a zoning change on the river across the county line and the landowners around it just sat back and watched it happen. Those folks are going to be faced with so many traffic issues just because they didn't show up at the zoning meeting and put their two cents worth in. They'll be raising a ruckus, but it'll be too late. I'm glad that's not going on around here."

"Do you know about any zoning changes down around Chance Cove?"

Polly spoke up, "That's where Madge Johnson's house is, isn't it?"

"Exactly," said Rock. "Are you friends with Madge?"

"No, I don't know her well, but I heard her son was going to be selling her house and I went by to look at it for my boy Frank and his family. It's listed through one of those Help-U-Sell realtors. The realtor told me somebody had already put down money for an option to buy it. He said Madge's son signed an agreement to hold off selling it for a month so these people could firm up their offer on buying another property nearby."

Bingo, thought Rock. "I haven't seen any other property for sale in there," he said.

"Me either," said Polly, "and believe me, I've been looking. That little house of Frank's is not big enough to cuss a cat in and what with Jenny expecting twins in November, they'll be all over each other."

"I'm out and about a good bit, Polly. If I see any For Sale signs go up, I'll give you a call right away so you can get a head start on checking them out."

"I would appreciate that Rev Rock. It's got to where the average Joe can't afford property around here anymore what with all the people from Charlotte movin' out this way. A fixer-upper would do just fine. Frank's right handy with a hammer and a paint brush."

"Polly, would you do me a favor?"

"If it's something I can do, I'll be happy to."

He gave her his card. "Call me if you hear of any proposed zoning changes out that way."

"Glad to," said Polly and Rock walked out the door and up the stairs to street level. The sun was a welcome sight after the darkness of the windowless basement. I would go stark raving mad down there, he thought.

***

It was 4 pm when Rock walked into the post office to check his box and buy stamps. Packages of bread in all sizes and shapes lined the counter along with two other customers. "Betty, it's been two days since I've been in this place and you've already turned it into a bakery. I knew the Postal Service was cutting back, but now they've got you selling bread." Betty looked at him from behind the counter with an icy stare.

"Don't you go carrying on and startin' somethin', Rev Rock. Can't you see I'm not in the mood to be trifled with?" Rock was getting ready to respond but Betty shook her finger at him. "Unh, uh – not another word! I can just see it now - they're gonna' call me the Bread Lady on top of my other titles. Today I've been the Dog Catcher, School Bus Messenger – can you believe that - the school called me and told me to go tell the bus driver when he passed by here that he left a kid at school. With my bad knee and I had to run flag down a school bus!"

Wanda Burns had walked in right behind Rock and was already laughing. "And don't you go putting that in your book, Miss Wanda. I just know you're gonna' have half the things I say and do in that book of yours – and I got all this bread to give out and here it is closing time – I think I'll just put a loaf in everybody's box - that's what I'll do. Here, catch," she said throwing a loaf at Rock and one at Wanda.

Rock was caught by surprise and missed his loaf, but Wanda caught hers like a football halfback. He fully expected her to run with it. "Don't be acting like it's a hot potato Rev Rock - it's perfectly good bread - day old, mind you, but perfectly good bread. It came from that new Publix up on the highway. Loraine Smith brought it by here on her way home. She runs that mission program over at the big Methodist church in Rock Hill and this much was left over from their soup kitchen today. Now what am I going to do with all this bread?"

"Well you could always give it to Louise Ledford for her chickens." At that, Betty threw a french loaf about the size of a baseball bat and almost as hard at Rock's head.

He ducked just in the nick of time. It was no wonder that people drove out of their way to the Park Place Post Office. Betty was better entertainment than a $10 movie ticket.

"I need to get her to preach my sermon," Rock mumbled as he picked up the bread and started to leave.

Joe Lowry, one of the elders in the church was standing at the door. "Our attendance would go up without a doubt," he teased as Rock walked out the door.

CHAPTER 19

For God has not given us a spirit of fear and timidity, but of power, love, and self-discipline.

~*2 Timothy 1:7 NLT*

Rock opened the back door that led into the kitchen. He had drifted off to sleep when he gave up trying to read the newspaper after Theo jumped into the middle of it on his lap. When Liz knocked, he jumped up, with Theo following him into the kitchen. "You've been asleep," she said. "I'm sorry I woke you." He gave her a sheepish grin.

"I didn't realize it showed."

"Well, your hair's a little mussed and you've drooled all down your chin," she said. He looked shocked and hastily wiped his chin. "I'm just kidding," she said with a grin. "I brought you some of the leftover soup I made yesterday and a loaf of banana bread." He loved her soup. "I'm leaving in the morning for the mountain cabin. I made Earl a loaf to take with me and my recipe makes two. I'm trying hard to cut back on bread and if I give it to you, I won't be tempted." Liz walked on in and put it on the table.

"Thanks. Can you stay while I heat up the soup? Then you can have a tiny slice with me over coffee; how about it?"

"Sure," she said, and sat down at the table while he

put the soup in the microwave.

"How long will you be gone?"

"Just a few days – I need to sweep out the cobwebs. I haven't been since I closed it up in October."

"Will you be back before Holly's surgery?"

"I'll try to." Their eyes met and held for a moment. Rock was the first to look away. He found himself wanting to beg her to stay.

He cut two slices of the banana bread and slathered butter all over his slice. The coffee was steaming in the mugs. "When do you resume your "Sonny" search?" she asked.

"So far, I only have the one lead and I may as well get on with it. I'm not looking forward to going all the way to Sparta to a livestock barn but they're having an auction tomorrow night so I'm going."

"It'll be fun," she said. "You'll probably come home with a pig to give Theo some company."

"Just commit me to the funny farm if I do." They both laughed, but there was a new feeling of timidity between them, an uncertainty of sorts.

***

There were only a few cars in the parking lot. The building looked sturdy enough. It had been someone's barn at one time. It had been patched up many times over the years with a lopsided stray board here and there, just enough to keep the elements at bay. As he stepped inside the open barn door entrance the air reeked with the pungent smells of a childhood memory – the memory of a week spent on a farm.

His best friend Craig went for a two week stay at his grandfather's farm each summer. One year he had invited Rock to come along. Rock was excited – he loved going to his own grandparents' dairy farm where he could fish in the pond all day if he wanted to. The first day had been full of hugs from Craig's grandmother. She hugged Rock just as fiercely as she hugged Craig not wanting him to feel left out. She had insisted that Rock call them Grammy and Pap just like Craig did. There were cookies and homemade ice cream and two nearby cousins had come over to play with them. What a wonderful way to live he had thought and went sound asleep with visions of playing and eating ice cream and cookies all week.

His dreams were dashed the next morning when Pap woke them up at 6:30 a.m. and told them to put on a long sleeve shirt. Rock protested that he didn't bring a long sleeve shirt since it was summer. "You can borrow one of Craig's" he said and walked out the door. After Grammy fed them breakfast, Pap gave them each a bucket and led them to the first rows of what seemed like an endless field of squash. The cousins were already there ahead of them. "There's buckets placed throughout the field," Pap had said. "When you fill one up, just leave it where it is and grab another. Joe will come fetch the buckets and put them in the back of the truck." He gave each of them a pair of work gloves.

"Why do I need these," Rock had asked.

"Just pick for a while without them and you'll know," said Pap grinning.

When the bucket bottom had been barely covered,

Rock had donned the gloves. The long stems on the squash plants were prickly and his hands and arms were on fire. He had rejected the long sleeve shirt Craig had offered him and now longed for it. When he laid his first bucket down, he looked for Tommy. He spotted him and the cousins what seemed like a half mile away, already on their third buckets. Determined to keep up, Rock picked as fast as he could. He was miserable. His arms and legs were itching and his clothes were wet from the dew on the squash. He wondered why Tommy looked so forward to visiting the farm each summer. At the end of the row he found a long sleeve shirt on a brown grocery sack where Tommy's Pap had left it for him. It looked like water in the middle of the desert to him.

By the end of the day he was ready to go home. By the end of the week, he had vowed if he ever got home, he would never come back. There were two things he vowed to avoid for the rest of his life. First, chickens - he was allergic to chicken feathers and sneezed so much in the hen house that Grammy made sure he didn't have to help with the egg gathering again. Second, cow pastures - he didn't like the feel or smell of fresh cow manure as his foot sank into it when he wasn't paying attention to where he was walking. The cousins had died laughing over that one. Rock kept his vow throughout his childhood. Each year when Craig asked him to go again, Rock gave one excuse after another.

"Why don't you go back?" his mother had asked.

"I'm allergic to chicken feathers," he had replied. She left it at that.

***

Rock saw a sign at the other end of the barn with an arrow pointing the way to the office. Goats were in wooden enclosures on his right. There was one horse in a stall near the goats. His swayed back was an indication of his age and Rock hoped he wouldn't end up in a glue factory somewhere. The chickens were protesting their new digs. They were stacked in wire cages and the roosters were crowing at the top of their voices still trying to compete and establish a pecking order. Rock looked for water in the cages, but didn't see any. It's hot as blazes in here, he thought and now he had to add the chickens without water to his worry list.

He walked into the office. There was one man behind the counter busy with a seller, entering his inventory of goats and birds into the computer. The brief walk beside the chickens had already made him sniffle and he grabbed a tissue off the counter. "May I help you," a sweet voice called out from behind the counter. A young girl no more than sixteen appeared out of nowhere. At Rock's startled expression, she grinned. "I was under the counter plugging in the calculator," she said. "Grandpa insists on still using one in addition to the computer." She held out her hand – "My name's Mindy, she said. Still smiling, she pointed to the computer. "Grandpa still doesn't trust those gol darned things," she said in a voice mimicking her grandfather. They both laughed.

"I understand - I've had my moments," said Rock. "But yes, maybe you can help me. I'm looking for Sonny Haywood - someone told me he works here." She gave him a curious look and seemed to be waiting for an explanation of why he was looking for him. When he didn't offer one, she answered him.

"Yes sir, he does but he hasn't come in yet this afternoon. He's due in at 5:30 but sometimes comes early." Rock looked at his watch – 4:27 – he would have to wait around another hour.

"I'll wait outside in the barn, but if I miss him, would you mind giving him my card. She looked at his card and smiled.

"Just look around out in the barn," she said. "You might find something you can't live without."

"The roosters look pretty interesting," he said. "If I wasn't allergic to feathers, I would get one for an alarm clock." She laughed. "Thanks again for your help," he said and turned to walk away. As an afterthought, he turned back around to her and smiled. "What happens if the calculator and computer don't match?"

"The problem is usually with the calculator, or the one who's using it," she said pointing to herself. "But I think he's beginning to come around."

"Good luck winning him over," he said and walked out the door.

The heat, the smell of the animals and the chicken feathers convinced him to wait outside in the truck. At 5:20, he walked back inside. More animals had arrived and the sounds had grown a little louder. There was a young man walking through the gate that led into the goat stalls. He closed it behind him. Rock leaned over the gate and called out to him. "Can you tell me where I can find Sonny?"

The man looked as puzzled as Mindy. "He's unstacking the crates of chickens to cool them down," he said. "He'll be out in a few minutes."

Rock wandered over to the front corner where someone had just brought in some rabbits and cockatiels. A young boy was feeding a big fluffy white rabbit bites of an apple through the cage. "Nice looking rabbit," said Rock. The boy gave him a huge grin.

"Yeah, my grandpa's going to buy him for me if the bids don't go too high."

"So that's how it goes? You bid on the animals?" The boy looked him up and down.

"Yes sir. You don't know too much about auctions do you, Mister?" Rock laughed and walked away feeling that he had been put soundly in his place. He started sneezing again as he walked back past the chickens. They had been moved right in front of where people were beginning to sit in the bleacher style seating area. As he watched people taking their seats, he felt a hand on his shoulder. He turned around and came face to face with a neck the size of a football offensive tackle. The man was at least six inches taller than him and was wearing a sleeveless t-shirt that showed off tattoos covering every inch of skin.

"I heard you were looking for me." The voice was as big and gruff as the man himself.

"Uh, yes - maybe," said Rock and found himself backing up a little. The man moved closer.

"Well, what is it? I've got to get to work."

Rock's allergies kicked into full gear and he started coughing. "Uh, you can get on back to work. I left a card in the office - you can call me later. I've got to get out of here – I'm allergic to chicken feathers." And he practically ran out the door. "So that was Sonny," he said to himself as he cranked up his truck, "the same Sonny that left Jack's truck in a drug neighborhood." A little voice inside him scolded, "Rock, you're being judgmental." He pushed the voice aside and wanted to kick himself for leaving his card. He hoped Mindy had lost it. He drove home feeling like a wimp.

CHAPTER 20

The rain was falling gently on the tin roof of the porch. Liz shivered as she watched the raindrops break the surface of the mountain stream in front of the cabin. She watched the pink and white rhododendron blooms heavy with rain fall into the water and float aimlessly by. She had forgotten last night to call Diane to open up the windows. The cabin had been musty when she walked in so she had spent most of the morning de-winterizing, airing out and restocking the pantry and refrigerator with the groceries she had brought up the mountain with her. She thought of the many times over the years that she and Ron had done these things together and since his death Diane had come over each Spring to help her open it back up for the summer. She hadn't been able to face it alone...until now.

The cabin had been in her family for years. Her mother and father had vacationed here from Florida before she was born and fell in love with the serenity of the mountains. They had bought several acres bordering the stream for a song and had sold it off in parcels over the years to their Florida friends. Each summer brought all the Floridians back to their cabins. Some stayed only a few days, but most spent the whole summer. Later on, her job as a school counselor had made it easy for her to spend the summer. Ron would come up on Fridays after work and stay through Sunday. It was a comfortable routine and they had loved it.

The good memories of the times they shared had finally started filling in the tiny holes in her heart where the grief had been settling. Now as she sat on the porch watching the raindrops end and the sun start filtering through the trees, she felt new growth in the heart that she had felt would never beat in perfect rhythm again. She had told everyone this trip was to air out the house, but there was so much more that needed airing out before she could go on living a full life again. It was here in these tall green hills that she felt closer to God and where she would seek Ron's permission to go on with her life.

The off-key whistling broke into her thoughts and she smiled as she looked up to see Earl riding his bicycle around the bend in the road. Earl was her caretaker of sorts. She paid him a small fee to check on the cabin throughout the winter months and to mow the grass during the summer. Earl still lived in the old home place of his childhood under the watchful eye of a younger brother who lived next door. He had been the victim of a logging accident when he was a boy and had suffered a brain injury that had left him with a limited mental capacity. He always had a smile on his face and a song in his heart. In the basket of his bicycle he carried a waterproof pouch with packs of juicy fruit gum which he dispensed to everyone he came in contact with. Equally dispensed were the words of wisdom from the other object he carried in the backpack...a worn Bible from which he had memorized dozens of scripture verses – verses that he quoted, never in any kind of order. He also quoted bits and pieces of prayers and doxologies that he picked up during the worship services he looked forward to every Sunday morning.

"The Lord be with you Miss Lisbeth" he said as he walked up the steps.

"And also with you, Earl," she said back to him. This was the greeting they always used each time they met. It didn't matter that it was normally used as a benediction – it was a blessing all the same.

Liz often thought of Earl as he had been as a child. He had been ten and she had been fourteen the summer before his accident. His younger brother Aaron had been his shadow that year but the roles reversed later as Aaron became fiercely protective of his handicapped brother. The local residents and the entire valley of summer residents looked out for Earl in the ensuing years. They grew accustomed to his gentle nature and quiet demeanor and never thought of him as being odd or eccentric – he was just Earl. But some of the newcomers to the valley were put off by him, complaining that it was unsettling to walk out on their porch with their morning coffee and find a boy in a grown man's body sitting in one of their chairs whittling one of his animal carvings. The Nicholson's who had moved into the Garrett's cabin had gone so far as to call the Sheriff's Department to have him arrested for trespassing. Joe Cobb had been the deputy on duty and he explained to them that Earl was harmless but if they wanted him off their property, he would tell him to stay away. "It's your loss though," he had said. "Earl has a wealth of wisdom to impart. He just has difficulty finding the words to tell it, so he uses Bible verses that he's memorized to try to make sense of each situation. From then on, the Nicolson's had made Earl feel welcome and their three-year-old grandson had started randomly quoting Bible verses as he played around the house.

"It could be much worse," said Tom Nicholson as Arthur at the General Store rang up his groceries. "It makes his Grandma much happier than the time he quoted me word for word when I hit my thumb with a hammer."

Arthur chuckled as he recalled a few times when he wouldn't have wanted to be quoted either.

***

Ron had enjoyed Earl's company as much as Liz. He had watched with fascination as Earl whittled pieces of wood into the most exquisite forest creatures. His carving of a fox had won a place of honor on their mantle above the fireplace. Ron's excitement grew as he saw piece after piece being finished and convinced Earl that his talent should be shared. He packed a few of his carvings in the SUV and he and Earl drove down the mountain to Asheville to a local crafts gallery owned by Margaret Hamilton. She was thrilled and put them on prominent display in the window. They sold out within a week. Since then, Earl had become somewhat of a celebrity in and around Rocky Falls and his neighbors looked at him with a new respect. Margaret often became frustrated that he wasn't producing as fast as she was selling. Ron would intervene. "These are masterpieces," he had told her. "Your customers can get junky little carvings at every roadside stand from here to Tennessee. These are one of a kind and you can't rush perfection." This had appeased her and the demand for Earl's work became even higher when she made them put their names on a waiting list.

Liz went into the kitchen and came back with two mugs – one with coffee and the other hot chocolate, Earl's favorite. He wasn't whittling today. He fiddled with the handle of his mug and glanced at her now and then as if he wanted to tell her something. She knew him well enough not to rush him. He had to have time to sort things through. He would stutter if he felt rushed so she just sipped on her coffee and waited. Finally, he spoke.

"Miss Lizbeth." He seemed to have gotten over his nervousness.

"Yes, Earl?"

"My carvings are all gone."

"Earl," she said with alarm. "Do you mean someone stole your carvings?" Even his miniature carvings were bringing around $50. The large ones, depending on the subject, sold for $200 or more. To have someone steal from this gentle soul was unfathomable. Ron had helped Aaron set up a trust fund with his carvings sales so that if anything happened to his brother, this small amount of money, along with Aaron's insurance would take care of Earl's basic needs. There was a separate account for Earl to spend as he wished but his only splurge had been for a new bell and basket for his bike – and enough Juicy Fruit gum to keep the dentists in Asheville in business filling cavities for every kid in Rocky Falls.

Earl shook his head and seemed to be struggling for words to express his thoughts. "No, Miss Lisbeth. I have them here," he held out his hands palms up. "But I don't have them here." He put his right hand over his heart and looked at Liz pleadingly. For a moment she was puzzled, but then understood.

"Earl, what you're saying is you just don't have your heart in your carvings anymore – is that it?" Earl nodded, pleased that she understood. "Is it because you feel that you have to make them now instead of carving them because you enjoy it?" He nodded again.

She did understand. It was like an author friend had recently told her that writing was a way of expressing herself, but when she had published her first book and then another, the demands of trying to pump out books to please the publisher became a burden and she no longer got the same joy out of writing.

The mountain air was clear and a little cool for early June. She reached for the afghan she had brought out earlier and wrapped it around herself. Such a peaceful morning she thought. She wanted Earl to feel that sense of peace.

"Earl, you know you don't have to make them to sell anymore, don't you? You can quit selling them at any time. I'll go down and tell Margaret that you're putting your business on hold until further notice and not to call you anymore. If you ever decide to sell again, you can call her."

Earl looked relieved and smiled at her. He held his hand over his heart again and let out a big sigh. Liz laughed. "That wasn't so hard, was it?" Somehow, she had known what he would do next. He pulled his knife and a small wood block out of his pocket and started whittling again.

Liz left him on the porch and went back inside to get another cup of coffee and to finish her cleaning. She knew how he felt. She didn't know exactly where her heart belonged anymore either.

CHAPTER 21

*A*nd my God will supply every need of yours according to his riches in glory in Christ Jesus. - Philippians 4:19 ESV

The air conditioning in Rock's truck was running full blast as he turned left onto Chance Cove Road. The combination of the high humidity and the dust kicked up by the two teenagers riding four-wheelers ahead of him made the air so thick you could cut it with a knife. The *For Sale* sign was still in Madge's yard – this time with a small sign underneath it - *Contract Pending*. Pending what? Pending how many residents they can con into selling to them, Rock thought.

The day before, it had become clear to him what this business of trying to buy the land on Chance Cove was all about. It had not registered when he had read in the paper a while back about the water park on the other side of the river and even when Polly mentioned it at the zoning office. But as soon as Cap spoke of it at their weekly gathering at the Feed and Seed Store on Monday, it hit him like a ton of bricks. They had added Cap to their group now and he sat on the step stool Junie had rounded up. "I'll be getting me a new view," he told the men. "They're gonna be building a water park right across the river."

"You ought to start you a little river boat business," Junie had said. "With a restaurant beside your house -

and you could shuffle people back and forth across the river to eat. Why, you could make a killin' doing something like that."

The others talked it over for a while discussing the possible business ventures Cap could go into. "I'm too old for that," he said. "Besides it would disturb the peace at my place."

Rock didn't say anything but he had his own thoughts on the matter and after a little fact gathering mission on Tuesday morning, he dropped by Cap's house.

"You want to go with me on a little trip tomorrow?" he had asked. Cap nodded. "Can you be ready by 9 a.m.?"

"Do I have to dress up?"

"Yep, Sunday's finest." Cap's face fell.

"Aww..."

He could have kicked himself for not thinking about Cork County's zoning applications. There was no fancy white car pulling out of Cap's driveway this time and Cap was waiting on the porch when he pulled in. Rock was fully expecting Cap to be dressed in just a fancier version of his signature overalls, but to his surprise, he had on a modest light weight grey suit with a red bow tie.

"You look spiffy today," Rock said as he opened the car door for the older man. Cap grinned, showing off his missing front tooth.

"You don't look half bad yourself," he said and fastened his seatbelt.

"Where are we going?"

"We've got almost a full day's ride ahead of us," Rock answered.

"Maybe I should'a packed me a picnic lunch."

Rock laughed. "I'm not going to let you starve," he said.

"Nope, I don't reckon you would."

"We're going to Florence and then to Columbia."

"All in one day?"

Rock nodded, "And we're going to have to push the pedal to the metal to get it all done."

"Is this old truck up for it?"

"I don't know, let's see." And Rock spun rocks out of Cap's driveway in much the same way the white car had done last week."

Cap was delighted. "If it wasn't so dusty, I would roll down the window and let the wind blow through my hair."

Rock looked at him and smiled. "What hair?"

Cap's hand went to the top of his head and mussed up the little bit he had. "These three right here!" Then he broke out in a big grin. Rock knew it was going to be a good day – Cap was laughing.

When they got back out on the highway, Rock detailed their plans. "We'll need to go through the country and hit the Beach Highway to Florence. We'll see Madge - I've already called her and told her we would be coming today. She invited us to have lunch in their dining hall - I told her we would. Then we'll take I-26 to Columbia. We could fill out the application online but I thought it might speed up the process if we showed up with our handsome faces." He glanced at Cap.

"My handsome mug, you mean," said Cap. He tilted his face up in the air and showed his profile and cracked up laughing again.

***

When Rock had left the Feed and Seed Store on Monday, he had gone by the hospital. Holly wasn't in the room - Jamie said she was downstairs for a scan. He waited for a while, but when she hadn't returned thirty minutes later, he left the hospital and drove to Beverly Hills. He spent a couple of hours with the children and when Rebecca asked him to stay for dinner, he couldn't refuse - especially when he saw Estelle's biscuits being brought out on a big platter.

On his laptop at home, he poured through information online and then made a phone call to Bob Clayton.

"Well, sure it's been done. There's all sorts of options. I did some legal work for the Dickerson family over in Flat Creek who wanted to develop their property into an equestrian subdivision with large fifteen to twenty acre lots. There was a good bit of undevelopable land - you know, with marshes and big gullies and such. They had researched and found that if they made a big common area with walking and riding trails while maintaining the wooded areas and fragile marshlands, they could apply for a conservation easement and prevent future development. They said that's exactly what their father would have wanted. There was a small creek running through the land that's full of those Carolina Heelsplitter clams which are on the endangered species list. Because of that tiny little clam, they didn't have any trouble getting the easement done. The wildlife will be protected and the buyers will have a beautiful property to enjoy. And it didn't hurt that the new property owners will have a huge amount of acreage that they own 'in common' that they won't have to pay property taxes on."

"Aha," he said, "endangered species." He told Bob about Chance Cove and the natural habitat it provided for the Great Blue Heron.

"By Golly, you might be onto something," said Bob. "I wouldn't be surprised if there were some Carolina Heelsplitters in the creeks that are flowing into the river. They're all over the place right in this area. I would start with the Wildlife Commission or The Nature Conservancy."

"The Nature Conservancy has an office in Columbia," said Rock. "The info I found online says that to date they've protected over 300,000 acres across South Carolina."

"Good place to start," said Bob. "Just be aware of what you're getting into. There are huge profits to be made off that land since it's right across the river from a water park. These real estate people are gonna' try to gobble up land on the river here and won't be too happy that someone's blocking their progress. You may have trouble getting the landowners to help in your efforts - they'll be offered more money than they've ever dreamed of having. It'll be mighty tempting for them Rock."

Polly's phone call the next morning confirmed Rock's suspicions. "A cluster development with a golf course, a marina and a large restaurant. You didn't hear it from me," she said and hung up. Rock spent the rest of the morning driving around Chance Cove.

Hilda Burnett opened the door when he knocked. "James is out back feeding the chickens. I'll go get him."

"Hmph," said James. "So that's what she was up to. That real estate woman paid us a call and said she was buying up all the land on the other side of the road from us and would like to buy ours too. She said she already had a contract on Madge's place and said it was in the bag for Cap's. She offered us $300,000 for our two little houses and our twenty acres of land. I told her right off that she was out of her mind. I guess she figured I didn't think it was enough money and she upped it to $325,000. I told her I would think on it but I knew something was fishy and she was lying through her teeth."

"What made you think that?" asked Rock.

"Because everybody knows Cap Price ain't ever gonna' sell his little paradise on the water."

Hilda spoke up. "We talked about it with our daughter Laura and her husband Jimmy. It seemed like a lot of money when she said it, but like Jimmy said, we would be hard pressed to find two houses and land as pretty as ours for $325,000. We just aren't interested in selling. This land is all we need and the only place any of us have called home. We're hanging on to it. It'll be passed on down to Laura and Jimmy when we're gone. If we ever did decide to sell it, it wouldn't be to Miss Hilton. She seemed nice enough at first but then she got pushy." My sentiments exactly, thought Rock.

Rock was surprised when James told him that Cap owned the prime spot on Chance Cove. He had a huge rectangular piece of land - almost three hundred acres which ran about four acres deep in a straight line right down the river. He grew his corn crops almost down to the river bank and during summer droughts would use natural irrigation from the cove that ran through his property. He was known to birdwatchers throughout South Carolina for giving them the opportunity to view the Great Blue Heron and Pileated Woodpeckers that lived and thrived in his woods. "Why, we have birdwatchers from all over the country coming in here with their big old binoculars and funny little hats."

***

Rock and Cap had made it to Florence in a flash. With it being a weekday, there wasn't much beach traffic and the pleasant conversation made the miles pass quickly. Cap had entertained him with bits and pieces of local history. His stories, like Park Place, were centered round the railroad that ran right through the middle of town. In fact, Park Place had acquired its name at the whim of a traveling railroad executive's fancy. It was a rural area like most of the railway stops he had encountered on his way South to Florida and stopped only because of the one industry there - the Ashland Brick Company. There was just a small covered train depot where Mamie Patterson sold apple fritters and coffee to the wealthy Northern passengers on their way to Florida. "This place needs a new name," the engineer had said to him when they stopped.

The community shared a name similar to a neighboring town just across the state border and it was confusing as to which station he should make his stops. The executive had become bored with what he called all the 'one horse wagon' towns on their stops through the South. He and a friend had been amusing themselves with a game of Monopoly in the plush railroad car and he said in jest, "Let's call it Park Place."

"Why Park Place?" the engineer had asked.

"It's one of those stops in Monopoly that you want to avoid unless you own it." His friend chuckled, the engineer didn't get the joke and a new town name was born. The engineer had re-named the stop Park Place on his schedule and the locals, thinking it sounded rather grand and that it had come from someone in authority, made it official.

***

Madge Johnson was in the lobby waiting when they arrived. She hugged Rock and then turned to Cap and gave him her signature kiss on the cheek. "Cap, you old rascal, you're gonna' put all these old codgers to shame the way you're all gussied up. I'm going to prance right into the dining hall on your arm and make every one of 'em jealous." Cap's back got a little straighter and he extended his arm.

"I'd be right proud to be your lunch date, Madge Johnson." She took his arm and Rock followed them through the double doors to have lunch.

Rock practically had to tear Cap away when it was time for them to leave. Madge had looked at him and batted her already flirtatious eyes. "Why have I never had the pleasure of flirting with you, Cap Price?" she asked.

"Because we were married," said an indignant Cap.

"Ah yes....and happily," she said. "I do miss my dear Frank - and I'm sure you miss Josie. She was such a sweet soul."

He nodded, "It's awful lonely in that old house."

"That's why I moved here," Madge said. "There's never a dull moment, but sometimes I wonder if I was a bit hasty in asking Billy to sell my house. Why I might just decide to up and move back since there's a good looking eligible man living up the hill."

"Who's that?" asked Cap, and then blushed when he realized she was talking about him.

Madge had jumped on the bandwagon when Rock had told her of the plans for the land. "Billy sent me the contract to look over," she said. "But I just haven't had the heart to sign it yet. He called me just last night and said the realtor who wanted to buy it was pushing him to get it signed."

"She's pushing everybody," said Cap. "I don't have any children to leave my land to but I love it just the way it is and I don't cotton to having someone destroy the quiet peacefulness of it."

"I'll call Billy tonight and tell him the deal's off," she said. "I'm not hurting for money and neither is Billy. Frank was frugal and made some good investments while working for the railroad." Rock knew this was true because of the generous amount he had left to the church in his will.

"She's a lively woman," said Rock as they made their way down I-26.

Cap looked over at Rock and grinned. "She's not too bad to look at either," he said. He put his hand up to his mouth and felt the hole where his tooth was missing. "Do you know a good dentist?" he asked with a slight lisp.

***

Kimberly Hough was sitting behind the counter of The Nature Conservancy when they walked in. "Let's go in my office," she said. They asked her a few questions and then got down to business. She was excited when Cap told her he was considering willing his land to The Conservancy. "You can donate the land now and still maintain control of it throughout your lifetime," she said. It's called a Life Estate and it allows you to live there with the understanding that upon your death, the title will transfer to a charity of your choice - in this case, The Nature Conservancy. Since this is a rather sudden choice, Mr. Price, I would recommend that you take the paperwork to your lawyer and discuss it with him and with your family before you make a commitment. But if you do decide to do it, we can have our sign up on your property within a week."

"No family other than a few distant cousins who live in Georgia," said Cap. "They don't even know where I live."

Rock spoke up. "What about the other landowners?"

"We can do this with or without them," she said. "The size of Mr. Price's acreage is more than enough. We've been paying close attention to that area and have it listed in the state registry as one of the natural nesting sites of the Great Blue Heron. He can forge ahead with his donation if that's what he chooses to do. It sounds as if the others have heirs involved. We can include their land as a protected zone even without them donating it. Somewhere down the line, they may want to sell it and they'll have every right to do so."

"What are the advantages of donating it now?" asked Cap.

"One advantage is that the Conservancy will have some control over other areas near the donated land. For instance, the water park that is planned across the river will have to comply with some noise restrictions so as not to disturb the Herons. It may even discourage them from building the park there. Another advantage is that you'll never have to pay property tax again," she said.

"Yippee! Those taxes kill me. But wait - what happens if I ever...uh - decide to get married again?" Rock didn't intentionally jerk his head sideways to look at Cap and drop his mouth open, but he couldn't help himself. Cap looked back at Rock and shrugged his shoulders, "Wha-at? I'm not quite ready to be put out to pasture yet. We never know what God's got in store for us, now do we?"

Rock winked at Kimberly as he spoke to Cap. "Well, no we don't. Do you have anyone in mind?" Cap grinned and shook his head. His own thoughts drifted to Liz. What plans did God have for him? God would have trouble letting him know - he was never still long enough to listen. He stood up and put on his jacket which caused Cap to do the same.

"I'm sure your lawyer can work that out for you, Mr. Price." Kimberly got up and shook Cap's hand and led them down the hallway. "We're very fast in getting these signs up. We want to get the word out that we're working on conserving nature throughout South Carolina and the United States."

True to Kimberly's word, after Bob Clayton's dealings with her were done, a small brown metal sign was erected at the entrance to Chance Cove with an arrow pointing down the narrow dirt road. It read, "Chance Cove: Protected by The Nature Conservancy of South Carolina."

"The news is out," whispered Bob Clayton when he shook Rock's hand after his sermon on Sunday morning. "You're a hero to many and a scalawag to a few," he said. Rock looked puzzled, but over the next ten minutes his hand was shaken vigorously by most of the members of the congregation as they filed out of church. He heard comments that made him even wonder if they were talking about his sermon.

"Good job," said Martin Harris as he clapped him on the back. Bo Evans gave him a thumbs up and said, "You 'da Man!" But the Westerly's, a father and son real estate team, avoided eye contact and headed straight for their car without saying a word.

Bob hung around and walked back to Rock's office with him when everyone was gone. "The real estate people are looking at it through the eyes of greed and you can't blame them - it's money out the window for them. The county commissioners are looking at it as a missed opportunity to fatten the coffers with property taxes. But the good thing is, everyone else thinks you're a superhero."

"Me? How do they even know I was involved?"

"Are you serious?" Bob looked at him with amusement. "Do you not know how the gossip mill works? Oh, I forgot - I guess you're more immune to it than most. People don't come right out and share gossip with a preacher, do they? There's a Bible verse in there somewhere about it," he said, pointing to Rock's Bible on his desk.

At Rock's crestfallen look, Bob said, "Don't fret over it, Rock. Jesus threw the money changers out of the temple. That's what the major players in this scheme are - money changers. They get inside information before it's made public, they buy land from innocent people offering them a little over market value, and before you know it your picturesque little village is just a sprawling suburb of a big city like Charlotte." Bob paused to see if what he said had sunk in. Rock's worried expression had softened. "And don't forget, if popular opinion counts, they're liable to vote you in as mayor next year."

Feeling a little better, Rock said, "Harvey McIntyre won't like being rooted out by the likes of me."

***

The gossip mills were working overtime on Sunday afternoon and continued over to Monday morning when Rock met his friends at the Feed & Seed. Larry Braswell was already talking when Rock joined his friends. Macie Fincher told Larry's wife that she was seated at a table beside the Hiltons and the Westerlys at Provisions Restaurant after church. Mary Jo was with her parents and pitching quite a tantrum for all the restaurant to hear. "That meddlesome man," she had said. "This was absolutely no business of his to get involved in! He didn't gain a thing by doing what he did!" Her mother had tried to calm her, but according to Macie "there was no calming that wildcat down." Jim Westerly looked embarrassed and had spoken to her in a whisper, but Mary Joe just picked up her Gucci handbag and stormed from the table. "I don't care if he is a preacher, I'll get even with him!"

"Strong stuff! What's a goochie handbag," asked Fred Laney.

Junie stood up and walked to the counter to wait on Tom Harmon who had come in to buy a hummingbird feeder for his wife's birthday.

"It's one of those fancy pocketbooks you have to go all the way to New York City to buy," he said. "Cost you about a thousand dollars."

Tom Harmon looked at the bird feeder he had picked out and then back to Junie. "What? I think I better pick out another one - what's so special about this one that it cost so much?"

Junie slapped his hands on the counter and laughed. "Not the bird feeder," he said. "The Gucci pocketbook."

"The wife don't want no pocketbook, thank the good Lord above - especially if they cost a thousand bucks."

"It's your lucky day," said Junie, "the bird feeder is only $14.50 plus tax." He rang it up and Tom counted out his money.

Rock could think of nothing to say as the boys were talking. He nodded his head and laughed at their jokes, but he felt sick to his stomach when he at last walked out the door and down the street.

May's Flower Shop was on the corner and May was putting a large bouquet of flowers in her delivery van. He spoke first and she waved. She looked at him as if she wanted to say something, but then changed her mind and looked down. He stopped at the door to the van and looked in. "Those hydrangeas are huge," he said, "and so blue. That's going to brighten someone's day."

She looked back at him with a worried look. "Rev Rock, I got an order in this morning to deliver some flowers to you, but I wouldn't do it."

"For me? Why me?" He was puzzled by her demeanor. "Who placed the order and why couldn't you deliver them?"

"Well, they were called in anonymously. The lady said she would send someone in to pay cash. It seemed a little fishy and I'm just not comfortable doing arrangements of black flowers. They're spooky looking, if you ask me."

"Probably just a joke," he said and tried to laugh it off, but the look on his face told the real story and anyone could tell he didn't find it funny.

CHAPTER 22

He was staring out the window of his office when the phone rang. It was Peter Braem.

"Rock, I wanted to let you know that Dr. Woods called last night - there was an opening for a surgery room today."

"That was fast. What time will she operate?"

"I tried to get in touch with you earlier but you didn't answer your cell phone. We transferred Holly early this morning to Charlotte and Dr. Woods just called back. She's already out of surgery and doing fine. It was just as we thought - the cancer was confined inside the kidney wall and she was able to get it all."

"Praise be to God."

"Amen! Rock, she'll be there a couple of days and then she'll be transferred back here."

"That's good to hear Pete, thanks for calling." Nothing like a little good news to put life in perspective, he thought. He got up from his chair and went outside. When he walked across the courtyard, he noticed the gate was open to the Memorial Garden. He latched it and started down the sidewalk that led to the house. The magnolia trees were in full bloom and he breathed it all in. The rich scent of the blossoms mingling with honeysuckle filled the air on summer evenings and wafted through the open windows on Church Street. Seven of the trees had been planted on the grounds of the church thirty years ago to celebrate the seven decades since the church had been built. The plan had been to add another each year, but someone finally realized that magnolias are not that easy to maintain so no more had been planted.

Before he walked up the steps, he stood back and looked at the porch. You couldn't really call it a porch. It was long and narrow - not wide enough for porch rockers, but there were two sitting there, looking out of place - one on each side of the door. He had sat outside on one from time to time, but he felt that if he rocked hard enough and long enough, they would just scoot him clear off on his head. There were a few shrubs that had been planted and some small trees, but they hadn't grown enough to provide privacy from the road. He always felt on display when he sat there. Nope, he definitely preferred the porch on the cottage. He started to open the door and noticed that the Presbyterian Women had been at it again. Just when he started to get used to one wreath on his front door, they up and changed it. It seemed to him they changed it at least once a month, but in reality, it was only changed with the seasons. The wreath for Spring had been nice with yellow bells and tulips – this one was filled with the rich purples and blues of hydrangeas, but they were dried, not like the fresh ones from May's Flower Shop. It was all a little too feminine for his taste, but the women worked so hard each season coming up with fresh ideas and colors that he didn't have the heart to tell them he would prefer no wreath at all. As he started for the door, he tripped over something. "Ah ha!" he said, and wondered how Mabel knew he had eaten the last of her jelly this morning. She must have been in a hurry. It didn't have her customary label with the little floral border and her name in the center. This must be a fresh batch, he thought. The wild blackberries were just beginning to ripen.

He opened the heavy oak door with its leaded glass panels. A combination of smells greeted him as he stepped into the foyer. The scent of lemon oil and pine cleaner was a dead giveaway that the Merry Maids had just worked their magic in the house. Rock wasn't a messy person by nature, but he appreciated the church's generosity in hiring a house cleaning service to clean each week.

Theo had heard the door open and close and peeked furtively out the door of the master bedroom at the end of the hallway. "Aha - sleeping on my bed again Theo?" Theo alternated between stretching his front legs out and then his back legs – then gave Rock a look of disdain.

Rock walked into the kitchen and peered into the refrigerator hoping for a miracle. If only Merry Maids provided a cooking service, he thought. Rock was a good cook, but cooking for one person didn't seem worth all the trouble. "Theo, pickings are slim to none in here," he said and pulled out a half can of cat food covered in plastic wrap. He put it in Theo's dish along with his Kitty Chow. The cat had never outgrown his love for the tiny niblets made for kittens and refused to eat the grown-up cat food. He watched as Theo nibbled at his food, and then turned back to the refrigerator. He checked the dates of the storage containers of food and threw some of them out. He opened the vegetable drawer and pulled out a bag of prepared salad and a tomato. He filled a salad bowl, chopped the tomato, drained a can of chick peas and sprinkled them on top. He topped it off with shredded cheese, bagged croutons and some bleu cheese dressing Liz had made for him. He poured himself a glass of iced tea and sat down by himself at the table.

"Ah, the life of a bachelor," he said with sarcasm to Theo. "Lord, thank you for this food and for the delightful companionship of my cat to share it with. In Your Son's name, I pray. Amen." Theo looked up at him expectantly. "No ham tonight, Theo," and he chewed on the bland, slightly wilted lettuce made palatable only by the homemade bleu cheese dressing.

***

He awakened to the smell of coffee brewing. For a moment, he wondered who could be in the kitchen. This was the smell that he woke up to when his parents were visiting. His mom seemed to always be one step ahead of him, even when he set his alarm to go off early. Then he remembered he had pulled out his instruction manual last night for the first time and programmed his coffee maker to start brewing at 6 a.m. and wondered why he had never thought of doing this before. He'd had another dream – this time he was in a boat drifting away from land. Liz was gesturing for him to come back to the shore and Jan was on an island in the other direction waving him to her. And Mary Jo Hilton was in the boat with him and had just pulled out the plug and was laughing. A psychiatrist would have a field day with that dream, he thought. He lay still for a few minutes until the enticing smell lured him out of his bed. He knelt and prayed, "Lord God, this is another day you have made. Let us rejoice and be glad in it." His prayer was simple and heartfelt. Although he didn't call each one by name, he lifted to the Lord his congregants, his friends and his family. He thanked God for his many blessings and said a prayer for Liz as she traveled and spent the next few days in the mountain cabin. As he slipped on his bedroom shoes, he heard a thump on the front porch – it sounded as if the paper carrier had hit the target this time instead of her usual custom of throwing the paper in the hedges or just past the driveway.

Theo's lazy meow greeted him as he poured his coffee into his favorite mug, the one Ron had given him for his birthday just a few months before he died. It was a custom designed mug with "Golf Buddies" printed on it. There were two golf tees – one tee was holding a golf ball and had the name Ron printed below it. The other tee was holding a rock instead of a golf ball. Rock's name was printed below it. Ron had been the better player and had tried to help Rock work on his swing when his ball landed in a sand bunker. He picked up a pebble from the bunker and held it in his hand.

"Just swing the club as if you were throwing a rock," he had advised. "Remember when you were a kid and would pick up a flat rock and try to skip it over water? Use that lower body motion and swing your club that way." He gave a mock demonstration with the pebble. To Ron's amusement but not the trio of golfers behind them, Rock took the pebble from him and threw it towards the next green.

"Like that?" he said.

"Just like that," Ron said and they walked on. The mug was near and dear to him. He chuckled as he looked at it now. He missed his friend.

Rock saw Mabel's jar of jelly sitting on the counter where he had left it the night before. There was only an end piece of bread left in the package. He put it in the toaster and got the butter out of the fridge. When he had slathered the toast with butter and jelly, he took his plate along with his mug of coffee into the study. "Let's pick up where we left off on our sermon," he said to Theo who had followed him. He put the plate and mug on the lamp table and gathered his Bible and notebook from his desk. He brought them back to his armchair, sat down and opened the Bible to the scripture he was using for the sermon. He read the passages over and then bowed his head in prayer. "Lord, your Word is here before me. Give me the insight to learn from it in a new light. Guide me in my preparation – then guide my mouth and the words that come out of it so that I may speak Your truth in a way that all will understand. I am Your servant, Lord; use me as You will. In Your Son, Jesus' name I pray. Amen."

He heard a crash and cringed. Not the mug! Theo was making a mad dash from the lamp table but the mug was still there intact. "Thank you, Lord!" he said out loud. The plate had landed right side up on the floor and surprisingly had not broken. The toast had also landed jelly side up on the floor beside the plate. Theo was busy licking the jelly off the bread right down to the butter underneath. "Theo, are you so hungry that you had to eat my toast? Okay, I'll feed you." He walked into the kitchen to throw away the toast and put the dish in the dishwasher. He cleaned Theo's dish and poured some fresh food. "Get your head out of the way old boy or you're going to be covered in cat food." Theo ignored him and stayed put. He swept up the bits that had spilled over Theo's head onto the floor. He opened the cabinet door and studied the contents. Finally, he grabbed a Pop-Tart and put it in the toaster. If all else fails, he thought, go for the Pop-Tarts.

"Reva, I'm working on my sermon from home this morning. If anyone calls, ask them to call the house number."

"Sure thing, Rev Rock. It's raining so hard, Mr. Linker's ducks are gonna need little umbrellas to get out in this mess. I'm only here because I have to be. I'll start working on the bulletin and you can just email me the scripture readings and the sermon title. If you get through in time, I'll print the copies and we'll be done with it early for a change. I sure don't want to be coming back in here tomorrow on my day off. I promised the grands I would take them to the dollar movies although it'll still cost me a fortune with popcorn, candy and co-colas. Did you know they won't let you take food and drinks into the movies anymore? Why, when my boys were little, we'd pop our own popcorn to take with us."

When she stopped to take a breath, Rock broke in. "Well, I'm sure you'll have fun with the kids Reva, and don't worry – I'll get it all to you in time for you to make copies. See you later." And he hung up before she started in again.

He had everything ready by 11:30 just as the sun was

breaking through the clouds. His internet service always went down with the rain. Since he couldn't email, he walked over to the church office to give the information to Reva. "I'm glad you came over. I wasn't lookin' forward to walking over to your house with this old bum hip today. This rain has got old Arthur all stirred up." Rock knew that Arthur was the name she gave to the arthritis that was constantly causing her pain.

"I'm sorry you're feeling bad Reva. Why did you need to come over to my house?"

"Mabel brought you a plate of fried chicken, a peach cobbler and a jar of that jelly you're so crazy for. I was going to bring it along to you shortly so you could have it for lunch. She said you had been pestering her about the jelly just this past Sunday so she fixed you right up." Rock's mouth was watering – the Pop-tart just didn't cut it this morning. The chicken was wrapped in foil and the cobbler was still steaming. The perfectly purple jelly was neatly labeled 'Mabel's Finest – Blackberry Jelly'.

"She must have forgotten she brought some over and put it on my porch yesterday. She didn't label it though," Rock said.

"Must be somebody else's jelly," said Reva with a chuckle. "Mabel don't forget nothin'!" He picked up the chicken and cobbler but left the jelly laying on the coffee table.

The paper carrier had picked a good day to hit the porch - it had landed in the rocking chair and was still dry. He poured a cup of cold coffee from the coffee maker and heated it in the microwave. He missed Liz's iced tea - it never turned out so good when he tried to make it. By the time he finished Mabel's chicken and peach cobbler, he felt like he could use a nap. While still at the table he picked up the paper and skimmed the front page. He read peacefully for a minute and then realized what was missing. Theo was not trying to sit down in the middle of the paper. The rain must have made him lazy too. Come to think of it, he hadn't seen much of him all morning. He must be sleeping on the bed again, he thought. He walked back to the bedroom but he wasn't there. He didn't come when he called so he walked back into the kitchen and to the door of the laundry room. Theo was curled up in the laundry basket where he slept each night. "What's up with you, Theo?" He reached down and rubbed him behind his ear. Theo raised his head and looked at him but still didn't make a move to get up. Concerned, Rock picked him up. He felt like a limp dishrag in his arms. "Uh oh, Buddy, something's not right," he said, and held him a little closer. His little heart was racing away. His nose, which was normally cold and wet was bone dry, lukewarm and caked with blood. Rock and Theo were out the door in three minutes flat and he was pacing the floor in the lobby of Bicketts Animal Hospital when Eileen Bickett opened the examining room door.

"It's a good thing you didn't wait any longer," Eileen said as she walked into the waiting room. Rock was standing near the door and watched as the vet's assistant gently lifted Theo from the table and took him out of the room.

"I'll get him prepped," she said.

"He's bleeding internally and we're going to have to

do a blood transfusion, Rock. Did you see any signs of blood on his bedding?"

"I didn't look at his bedding, but I noticed some blood in the cat carrier when we took him out. Rock's voice was shaky. "Will he be okay?" Aileen met his gaze.

"Rock, I took some blood samples to be sure, but I suspect some type of poison from all the symptoms he has. Just from a quick examination, I don't see any signs of a tumor or any other medical condition that would cause concern. The lethargy, racing heart and internal bleeding are all symptoms of poisoning. Is he an outside cat?"

Rock couldn't believe what he was hearing. "Poison? No, he rarely goes outside. Sometimes he walks outside with me when I'm watering the lawn or trimming the hedges, but it's been at least a week since he's set foot outside the door."

"What about a cleaning service? Do you have someone cleaning your house?"

"Yes, but they use non-toxic cleaning supplies. It's one of their selling points."

"Exterminators?"

"Not recently. The exterminator calls ahead and I take Theo to the neighbor's house when they're scheduled."

"I'm going to send his blood samples and some of the contents we drew from his stomach to be tested and then we'll know more. I've put in a rush for the test results to come back. Meanwhile, after the transfusion he will be hooked to an IV to keep him hydrated and we'll monitor him carefully. Don't worry Rock - I think you got him here in plenty of time."

Reva was sympathetic when he called to tell her he would be unavailable for the rest of the day. "Poisoned! How could he be poisoned right in your own house?" Don't you worry 'bout a thing here. Do you want me to start a prayer chain by email for Theo?"

"Let's not do that right now, Reva. I'd rather keep it under wraps for a while." He wasn't sure how his congregants would respond to praying for a cat, but he had already said his own personal prayer. He also didn't want the fact that Theo had ingested poison to get out until the test results came back. As in all small towns, stories were often embellished with each telling and before you knew it, there would be rumors that every cat in town was in danger. Maybe even a conspiracy theory that there was a cat hater out there lurking behind bushes to grab your cat. Well, they may not go that far he thought, but still.... No use feeding the rumor mill.

"Well I for one am going to pray for that cat - poor little thing!"

"Thanks Reva, I do appreciate your prayers. I'll talk to you in the morning."

He paced back and forth across the room trying to think of what Theo could have come in contact with – anything new that he could have brought in the house. Theo was curious and loved to carry things around in his mouth. He was always stealing pens from his desk and he had once retrieved a printer cartridge from the trash can and was carrying it around in his mouth. He was especially fond of plastic. If he found a drink bottle cap, he would bat it around for hours before losing it under the furniture. But plastic wasn't poisonous, was it? He didn't think so.

He thought again about the exterminator. He had been specific in his contract with warnings not to spray around the house until he could get Theo out. On those occasions, Liz would let him stay over with her until the twelve-hour danger period was over. But maybe they had a new worker that didn't pay attention to the orders. He checked his cell phone for their contact number but he didn't have it. A phone directory was on the counter so he went over and looked through the yellow pages, found the number and called.

"Reverend Clark, we have the manse and the church office on a quarterly schedule. It's been six weeks since we treated them – they were done at the same time. We only treat for termites so there's very little danger, if any, for you or your cat."

"Do you leave any kind of ant or bug bait that he could find?"

"No sir, but if you find any bugs or ants let us know and we'll add that to your service. I've got your file right here in front of me and we do have it flagged. A serviceman won't be assigned the job unless we have verbal confirmation from you that your cat's not in the house."

"Okay, thank you for checking. I'm just trying to cover all bases."

"You're welcome Reverend Clark – I hope and pray that all will be well with your cat."

Merry Maids – he went back to the counter and looked up their phone number in the directory. "No sir, we haven't changed cleaning products. We use all eco-friendly products, nothing that would be toxic to a cat. We don't even use chlorine bleach as most other cleaning services do."

He went back to his chair puzzling over what to do next. Eileen walked into the waiting room and approached a young woman on the other side of the waiting room. He had seen her walk in earlier and had marveled over the size of the cat she had in the carrier she was holding. Seeing her struggle with the weight of it, he had gone over to help her, thinking it was a dog inside. "He's a Maine Coon breed," she said when he expressed his surprise at how large the cat was.

"He's beautiful," he had remarked.

"He's here for his shots," she said. "He loves Dr. Eileen's treats so he doesn't mind the visit at all." The big cat was calm – not the slightest bit skittish.

Eileen and the young woman glanced his way. They talked for a short while and the young woman looked at him again and nodded her head in assent. Eileen motioned him over. "Rock, this is Carla Adkins. She's the owner of Rocky, the big cat you saw come in earlier. She said you helped her get him in the door."

"Rocky, nice name," Rock smiled and offered her his hand. "I'm Rock Clark, it's a pleasure to meet you."

"Likewise, Mr. Clark" – she shook his offered hand with a firm grip.

Eileen continued, "Rocky's a big healthy and sweet boy, Rock. I think, and Carla agrees, that Rocky would want to help save Theo's life by being a participant in the blood transfusion."

Rock's face showed the emotions he had been trying

to mask since he'd walked in with Theo. A wayward tear rolled down his cheek, then another. The floodgates were open. Carla and Eileen quickly followed suit and the receptionist ran over with a box of tissues. The four of them held hands and Rock offered up to a gracious God a plea for the health of Theo and for Rocky, the hero of the day.

"You can both go home," Eileen said as she gave each of them a hug. This will take several hours and we will want to keep Rocky overnight and Theo will be with us for a few days. Rock hated to leave Theo, but he knew it would be no use to ask to stay. Closing time for the clinic office was 5:30 and it was now a little after 5. "I'll call you both just as soon as the transfusion is over."

As Rock and Carla walked to their cars, Rock once again thanked her. "I know this could be risky for Rocky," he started. She put her hand on his arm. "Don't even think about," she said. "As soon as Eileen approached me, I knew it was the right thing to do. I would only hope that if Rocky was ever in Theo's shoes, someone else would make the same decision."

"You're an angel," he said...and meant it.

He drove around for a while trying to make sense of the situation. Why would someone try to poison an innocent cat? Maybe they were jumping to conclusions and it would end up being some sort of viral thing. Eileen had seemed very sure of her diagnosis though. He parked in the driveway without opening the garage door and walked up onto the porch. He had just picked up his newspaper a few hours earlier, but it seemed much longer.

The paper was on the kitchen table right where he

had left it along with his dirty plate and fork. The chicken and cobbler were still on the table. In his rush to get Theo to the vet, he'd not thought about putting it in the refrigerator. The cobbler would be fine. The chicken looked tempting to have for dinner, but he didn't want food poisoning. Regretfully, it would have to go in the trash.

He walked into his bedroom wishing it had been a bad dream and Theo would be asleep on his bed. The answering machine was beeping and the light was flashing.

The message was from Reva. She had brought leftovers from dinner and put in the refrigerator in the church office. "I know you won't think about eating with all that's on your mind," she said. She knows me well, thought Rock as he remembered his cupboard was bare except for the cobbler. Not even a slice of bread, he thought, remembering that his last slice had gone in the trash after Theo had knocked his plate off this morning. He shouldn't have had much of an appetite after the big lunch, but he did. The house was lonely without his cat. He took the trash bag out to the bin and found himself shutting the back door and walking down the path toward the office and the refrigerator. He had forgotten to turn the security light on in the back of the house, but the one at the office was on so he didn't have any problems seeing.

He passed the well-worn path that led to Liz's cottage and felt a pang of loneliness. No lights were on – it was dark and lifeless and held no appeal to him now that Liz was gone. It gave him a start to realize that he missed her so much and found himself longing for a glass of her sweet iced tea and their comfortable companionship sipping it on her porch. Was it just the camaraderie he was missing? As he thought about her smiling brown eyes and teasing mannerisms, he felt a stirring in his heart – an almost desperate desire to see her. "Whoa," he said out loud. "Where is this coming from?" He opened the office door and tried to clear the thought out of his mind. "I don't have time for a relationship," he said emphatically and the walls of the dark empty office echoed his words. He flipped the light switch, walked over to the fridge and pulled out the container Reva had left. It was a pot roast with potatoes and carrots and he felt his appetite return. She had left a note with instructions on how to heat it. "I'm sorry there's no onions," she wrote, "they give Walter indigestion." Walter eats like a king, he thought. He heated it up in the microwave and sat eating it at his desk alone. Once again, a feeling of loneliness engulfed him. Maybe a relationship wouldn't be so bad after all.

The phone rang at 9:44. He had been trying to concentrate on the prayer requests that had come in through his email correspondence. Eileen's voice was at the other end of the line. "It was a long procedure, but Theo and Rocky are resting well." Rock held his breath waiting for her to go on. "Theo's not out of the woods yet, Rock, but I'm very hopeful." That was what he had been waiting to hear. Hope - all creatures on earth should have it, he thought. Without it, there's nothing but despair.

Eileen went on, "I pumped his stomach and now that his blood is clean, there's no poison left in his body. This was hard on him, but being a healthy cat to begin with was in his favor. He's sedated so he'll sleep all night."

"How about Rocky?" He had worried about Rocky. The poor cat had gone to the vet in all innocence thinking he was going to get a few shots and some treats and he ended up flat on his back with a needle sucking his blood away. Carla had been kind to agree to the procedure.

"Rocky's just fine. I told Carla she could pick him up in the morning – he'll just be tired for a day or two."

"Eileen, I've gone over every scenario in my head on how he could have been poisoned and I've come up empty. We've ruled out cleaning products and the pest control service hasn't been by in over a month. This is killing me – if I don't know where he got it, how can I be sure he won't get into it again."

"Has he eaten anything different? Sometimes spoiled food can cause digestive problems, but not this serious."

"No, same cat food as always. I wash his water and food bowl every day. And no, he hasn't eaten anything different unless you count Mabel's blackberry jelly. He licked a little off my toast this morning." Eileen laughed.

"Half the town would be sick by now if it was Mabel's jelly. She must sell at least a hundred jars at the church bake sale each year."

"I've eaten my share," he said and thought about the two jars he now had – the one at home he had just opened and the new one at the office.

"Check with your neighbors and maybe even your own driveway to make sure you're not losing antifreeze from your radiator. It smells sweet and it's very toxic to cats and dogs."

"That's a thought," said Rock. "I had some radiator trouble a while back. I'll check the garage floor and I'll talk to the neighbors." Once again it struck him that one particular neighbor, the nearest of all, was not home and he decided that he would call her as soon as he got off the phone and tell her about Theo.

"Don't worry too much for now, Rock. We'll know for certain when we get the lab tests back on Monday. Why don't you come by in the morning and visit with him for a little while. He'll still be getting his nourishment from an IV for the next day or two and then we'll see how his tummy can handle a little food." Rock thought about Theo with tubes hooked everywhere and wondered how terrified he would be when he woke up. As if reading his mind, Eileen added, "We'll keep him sedated so he won't be stressed." He thanked Eileen for everything she had done and hung up fast so she wouldn't hear the sniffle that was shaping up in the back of his throat.

***

Rock hadn't heard from Liz since she left for the cabin. She had said she would be gone for a few days but now he was wondering what she meant by a "few days." He had treated her going away casually – she had been gone many times before and it didn't bother him and he never kept track of the length of her stay. Since Ron's death, she sometimes only stayed through a weekend, but last year she had stayed a couple of weeks at a time. Now he was hoping that a few days meant maybe three days; that way she could be home as early as tomorrow. He had planned to call her, but now he wasn't so sure. He didn't want to disturb her. Her time at the cabin was almost sacred. Should he, or shouldn't he? He decided to wait.

In his emotional state, he wasn't sure he could mask his eagerness to see her.

CHAPTER 23

The sun made its way over the mountain and was filtering through the trees when Liz took her coffee and Bible onto the porch and sat on the swing. She reached in the storage chest she kept on the porch and pulled out a towel and a small blanket. The night air had brought in moisture that had settled on all the furniture. After drying off the swing, she sat down on the blanket.

She had spent the day before going through cabinets and drawers and was surprised at the number of things she found that still brought back vivid memories of Ron. She had planned to use this as a cleansing week - a soul cleansing as well as a cabin cleaning. All the little things she hadn't had the heart to give away the preceding year - things she had no need of - she planned this time to box them up and take them to a local charity store that helped sponsor a battered women's shelter. There were two boxes - things to keep and things to give away. She kept putting things in the giveaway box and then taking them out. She had taken Ron's yellow rain parka in and out of the charity box so many times she thought she might wear it out before anyone had the benefit of wearing it. She had her own matching parka so she had no need for it, but it rained so much here in the valley that an overnight guest might use it. But when did she have overnight guests? Donna Harper, one of her teacher friends, had sometimes spent a few nights during summer breaks from school and her cousin from Atlanta always came for a week in August, but there had been no male guests since the last time Rock visited when the three of them were all together. She left it out. The next time he visited.... She put it back in. He wouldn't be comfortable visiting without Ron here, she thought.

She found the mug she was now holding at the back corner of the kitchen cabinet and chuckled when she pulled it out. I can't throw that one out, she thought. Ron had matching custom mugs made – one for himself and one for Rock. She could still picture the good friends laughing over the two golf tees portrayed on the mug. One tee was holding a ball and the other a rock. She couldn't remember the story behind it but the memory was a pleasant one. She looked at the mug now, Rock and Ron – how could she have such strong feelings for one when the memory and love for the other was still so overwhelming? She wondered if Rock still had his mug, and if so, did he still think of his old buddy when he used it? The shirt she was now wearing under her robe was another she had put in and out of the box. It was a well-worn jersey with Ron's alma mater embroidered on the back. A year earlier it had brought her comfort wearing it as a nightshirt. Now it just seemed to confuse her. Her mind should be on Ron - he had been everything to her. For almost two years now she had felt that she was in a fog, with grief seeming to suck the life from her very being. Lately the fog had started to lift and it was Rock's face she saw pulling her out of the darkness and away from her grief. She put her empty cup on the porch rail, pulled her legs up under her and opened her Bible. She had been reading the book of John and opened it to her bookmarked page. She had highlighted a verse at some point, but today it seemed as if God was speaking to her through the verse as she read it again - Chapter 8, verse 12 - *Then Jesus spoke to them again, saying, "I am the light of the world. He who follows Me shall not walk in darkness, but have the light of life."*

She put the Bible on the swing beside her and looked up. The tree leaves had turned a sparkling silver as the sun made its way through the thicket of wild rhododendron and she felt God's presence and heard his voice. "My daughter, have faith. Follow me and I will lead you out of darkness and into the light." There was no doubt in her mind that it was God's voice. Her faith had been tested until she had wondered if she would ever really feel God's presence again. She had prayed for guidance and here it was, plain and simple - just follow Me. She sat there for a moment soaking it all in and felt a renewed spirit when she headed back inside. The phone was ringing when she opened the door. Rock, she thought, and hurried to pick it up. It was Peggy. "Let's go down to Asheville and have lunch today."

Liz didn't have time for lunch dates if she wanted to get back home anytime soon - she still had boxes to fill to take to the charity resale shop and she also needed a little quiet time to sort through her new feelings. But she had not spent much time with Peggy this trip and didn't want to disappoint her. She was beginning to feel at peace here. Why spoil it by going home to uncertainty?

"Tell you what - if you'll come over and help me finish packing this stuff up, I'll have time to go with you to lunch. We'll load the boxes in my car and drop them off on our way."

She decided to call Rock to let him know she may be gone a day or two longer. She hesitated to call his cell phone because she never knew when he would be in a hospital room or in a counseling session. She called his home phone and left a message. He was good about checking his messages.

The job went much faster with Peggy helping her. This time around, there was no taking things back out of the box. "These few days have been a cleansing experience in more ways than one," she told Peggy. Her friend looked at her and much to her delight could tell that the old Liz was back.

Peggy had brought her Elvis CDs and they both crooned along to the music until 'A Big-a Hunk o' Love" started playing - it was Peggy's favorite. She jumped up and held an imaginary guitar and started singing. Her gyrating hips and jiggling knees brought on a fit of laughter and they sang even louder.

Mac Ledbetter was downstream fishing and told his wife later that Peggy and Liz were having a party and that house must have been full of people with all the loud music playing and laughing going on. "I think they musta' been drinking," he said.

She fussed at him and said, "That's how rumors get started, you crazy old coot. They're just havin' some girlfriend time. It's about time we heard laughter from that cabin again. I was beginning to think we never would."

"Hmph," he said.

"You're just jealous you weren't invited."

CHAPTER 24

Bickett's Animal hospital hadn't yet opened when Rock pulled into the parking lot, but a few minutes later, Cindy, the receptionist opened the door. "I saw you waiting and thought you would want to come on in and see Theo," she said. The smile on her face told him that his cat had made it through the worst of it. "Dr. Bickett isn't in yet - she was here until after midnight. Dr. Marsh is handling her patients this morning." Rock knew that Theo had been the cause of Eileen's late-night hours. "Theo's been stirring around this morning, but he's acting like a grumpy old bear."

"That's his normal personality," Rock said. "Don't take offense."

Cindy laughed. "Come on back."

Theo had looked pitiful and weak, but as Cindy had said, he was well enough to be grumpy. He calmed down when Rock stroked his back. "He's getting all he needs in this drip line," Dr. Marsh pointed out when he walked in. When Eileen gets here, she may decide to take him off of this and see if he'll drink water on his own. I think he's going to be fine." That was what Rock wanted to hear.

***

When he walked into the post office to pick up his mail, Wanda Burns was standing in front of the counter. She had her usual pen and notebook and seemed to be trying to coerce Betty into talking to her. "Come on Betty, I'm not going to put anything bad in my book about you. It's just that I'm writing about a small town and every small town has a post office, you know? I just want to know some of the best things and some of the worst things that have ever happened to you while you were on the job."

"Hmph...I thought you would have finished that book by now."

"It takes a long time to write a book, Betty. You can't just finish it in weeks or even months. As a matter of fact, I've thought about writing about the beach instead. I'm going to be using a friend's beach house for the rest of the summer." She winked at Rock. "It's too hard to get any good stories around here, especially when you tell everybody not to talk to me because I'm writing a book."

"If you don't quit hanging around here trying to put words in my mouth Miss Wanda, I'm going to tell everybody you're one of the worst things that ever happened to me." Wanda knew she was teasing and kept quiet for a minute – she knew Betty was thinking it over. And true to her thoughts, Betty started talking. Rock waited – he was curious too.

"Well, there were two worst things," she started. "I was pretty new on the job at the post office and I was the low man on the totem pole, if you know what I mean?" Wanda nodded and started writing. "They sent me up to Charlotte to train me and I was in the back with a bunch of men..."

Uh oh, where is this going, thought Rock. She continued, "Well anyway, I was emptying the mail pouches so we could start sorting and getting the mail out to the mail carriers for delivery. I picked up this shoebox size package and noticed it had some sort of dust all over it. Then I noticed I had dusty stuff all over my hands. Thank goodness, I was wearin' an apron or it would have got all over my clothes too." Betty shuddered. She was giving one of her best performances.

"Oh my! What was it?" asked Wanda. Since it was one of Betty's worst things, thoughts of poisonous powder or illegal drugs came to Rock's mind.

He and Wanda waited, holding their breath. "Just hold your horses, I'm gettin' to it," Betty said. "Well anyway, I turned the box over and what was written on the outside of that box was enough to turn me to stone." She shuddered again.

"Salt?" said Wanda. Rock couldn't help but laugh knowing what she was thinking. Wanda was known as the Blonde of Park Place because of her naivety and absentmindedness.

"No-o, not salt," said Betty sounding exasperated. "Whatever made you think salt?"

Rock spoke up. "She's thinking Lot's wife being turned into a pillar of Salt."

Betty rolled her eyes. "Well, I never! Let me get back to my story."

Please do, thought Rock.

"Well, anyways - when I read the writing on that box, I threw that box down and I let out a bloodcurdling scream." Now that she had both Rock and Wanda's attention, she paused for effect. Rock looked at Wanda. Her eyes were wide open and her mouth was as well.

Betty was enjoying her own story.

"What did it say?"

"Don't rush me. It takes time to tell a story right." She gave Wanda her signature look and pulled her stool up a little further to the counter.

"Well, all those men – they came a' running back there thinking maybe I had seen a snake or a rat or something. They looked at the box and they just laughed at me."

Wanda was getting impatient and had quit trying to write anything. "Well, what was it!"

"Cremated Remains – that's what it was marked!" Betty said with satisfaction. "And I had the ashes all over me. Now if that don't give you a creepy feeling, nothin' will. I ran to the bathroom as fast as my feet would take me and washed my hands."

"In a shoebox?" asked Wanda.

"Yes ma'am," Betty replied and Rock walked into the lobby forgetting what he had come in for. Oh yeah, he thought, I just came in to say hello to Betty. He shook his head – you could never just come in to say hello to Betty. He walked over to his box and got his mail. Nothing but bills.

Reva had asked him to check the box for the church so he opened it with his key. Not much in here, he thought. There was an invoice from AirTherm for work on the air conditioning unit along with the electricity bill and something else. That's strange, he thought - a hand addressed envelope that had the correct address for the church, but it was addressed "To Preacher." There was no return address. He opened it up and a crudely written note fell out of the envelope. He stooped to pick it up and tried to read it. The handwriting had been disguised so that it was almost illegible, but he finally made it out. "You'll regret snooping around in other people's business." He felt like Betty must have felt with the ashes – he wanted to wash his hands.

CHAPTER 25

Rock looked in the glass door and saw that Betty and Wanda were still talking. It wouldn't do to pull Wanda in on this - as Betty said, she would write it down and put it in her book. He would ask Betty later if anyone suspicious had been in - she was active in the neighborhood crime watch and not much got past her. Reva had only checked the box once last week so the envelope could have been in there for a few days. He held it carefully between his thumb and index finger in case it still had fingerprints, but then half laughed as he realized he was acting like a Sherlock Holmes. He started to walk to the police station but decided against it. The note was probably a prank - maybe he had stepped on someone's toes with his sermon on Sunday, but he couldn't for the life of him think of anything controversial he had said.

He took a shortcut from the post office down the side street at the back of the church and walked through the back gate. "Please God, let her be home," he said aloud. Her car was not in the driveway and the house was locked up tight. The roses needed watering, so he went around back for the water hose and gave everything a good soaking. Liz had told him he could sit on her porch whether she was home or not, so he walked up the steps and sat in the rocker he had begun to think of as his own.

It only took him a few minutes of rocking to realize that the porch alone was not what kept him coming up the little path. And it's not the tea either, he thought. "A few days, my eye," he said, and walked down the steps with his shoulders sagging, grumbling and muttering under his breath. He was glad to see that Reva had not made it back to the office. He needed some quiet time and he needed to figure out what to do about the ugly thing sitting amongst his mail like a hot potato.

He couldn't concentrate - it seemed a culmination of everything that had happened over the last week was weighing him down. Jess Hamilton's contact information was in his cell phone - he called the number but it went into voicemail. He left a brief message. "Jess, I received a strange letter today that I think you should see. I'll bring it down to the station later."

His thoughts drifted back to Liz - he would like to run all this by her. She would know what to do. Why had she not come home? From his office, he could see the flower lattice that protected the porch from view. He could almost see beyond the lattice her sitting there, right where he had just been, book in hand reading contentedly and he could imagine her smiling a big welcome as he walked upon the porch - unlike the feeling of abandonment he had felt just a few minutes ago as he sat there alone. He thought about how her smile was contagious and how her eyes twinkled when she talked - emerald green eyes with little flecks of brown throughout. The way she flicked her hair back when it fell forward into her face - the warm brown color of it - so silky and smooth looking, it made him want to touch it.

He tried shaking off the daydream. He realized he was being selfish - she needed this time. If he didn't have so much going on, he would hop in the car and go surprise her. The mountains would be cool and.... "Back to earth, Rock, old boy," he said aloud. "You don't need to be going down this path!

He walked to the front office and sat on the sofa overlooking the courtyard. The brick courtyard was a masterpiece, designed by brick masons and craftsmen of the early 20th century using hand-molded kiln dried brick. The historical records told the story. Ashland Brick had donated all the brick used to build the church and the courtyard - the Ashland family had been charter members. All the brick was red - made from the Carolina Piedmont red clay, but right in the center was the design of a cross made up of bricks molded from the blue clay found along the banks of the Catawba River. This was the same clay that the native Indians had used for centuries in the making of their pottery pieces. There had been a few decaying bricks in the courtyard over the years, but there was plenty of old brick for repairs - saved when old buildings had collapsed and sitting in the backyards or basements of the families of Park Place.

The oaks on the property were the same age as the brick, being planted as seedlings when the church had been built. Across the courtyard was the bell tower. No matter how many times he looked at the structure, its architectural beauty never failed to impress him.

He moved his laptop and briefcase to the coffee table and settled on the sofa. He heard it before he saw it - the distinct roar of a motorcycle as it came to a grinding halt in the parking lot beside his truck. The huge burly figure of a man that was riding it seemed vaguely familiar. The vast array of tattoos on the arms and shoulders as he dismounted and took off his helmet confirmed his fears - it was the large hulk of a man, Sonny Watson from the livestock auction. It made him feel a little better that it was a Honda Gold Wing instead of a Harley, but the feeling went out the window as Sonny slung something over his shoulder. Oh my stars, he thought - a gun case. He knew he should get up and lock the door, but he froze in place. He looked down at the mail on the coffee table - the letter! He rushed to lock the door but like a movie in slow motion, by the time he got there it was too late - the handle was already turning.

CHAPTER 26

Reva glanced at her watch as she took the hot pie dish from the trunk of her car. She was a half hour late getting back from lunch but she knew Rock would forgive her when he pulled the foil off the hot, steaming peach cobbler she had just taken out of the oven. She smiled as she thought about his reaction. That boy is a fool over peach cobbler, she thought. "It's 'bout time he gets himself a wife - I'm tired of being a wife to two people," she told Walter as she was walking out the door of her house.

"You keep feeding him like this, he won't need to get a wife." He smiled tenderly at his wife of forty-five years. "But you wouldn't have it any other way. You love that boy like he's your own."

"Somebody's got to see that he eats proper," she said. "He's as skinny as a rail. Miss Liz - now she would take good care of him. If he could just see what's good for him!"

"Oh, he'll see one day - without any interfering on your part. If she's the one the Almighty's got picked out for him, he'll figure it out."

"Hmph! That boy needs a little poke with a cattle prod, yes he does. Close the door behind me Walter - I've got my hands full."

She had parked in her parking place and popped the lid of the trunk before she got out of the car. She used her oven mitt to pick up the hot dish and had to balance it to shut the lid. Her 'Be Happy' licence plate rattled and made a mental note to ask Walter to tighten it before it fell off. As she balanced the dish, she looked toward the cottage and thought about Liz. She's taking her sweet time coming back from the mountain house, she thought. Maybe she's planned it this way and is doin' a little conniving of her own. She smiled at the thought.

Her car was on the right-hand side of Rock's truck and as she walked behind it toward the kitchen door, she noticed the motorcycle. "Now what kind of visitor we got here?" she muttered. There were no appointments filled in on his calendar, but that didn't mean much; Rock had an open-door policy and people were always dropping by when they saw he was at the office.

The dish was still hot so she laid it on the bumper of Rock's truck while she dug out her keys. She would let herself in the back door so as not to bother Rock and his visitor, so she left the dish where it was and went to unlock the door. The blinds were open and she glanced inside.

"Lord, have mercy!" She didn't mean to say it so loud but it startled her. She quickly turned around and walked back where they wouldn't see her. Rock was sitting on the sofa and a big man was sitting opposite him on the armchair. He had on a sleeveless tee shirt showing off what she had heard the young kids call 'skin graffiti' and he was holding something across his lap - a shotgun.

"Lord, what am I gonna' do?" she said aloud. "Times like this is when I need a cell phone - but no use worrying about it now." Thoughts filled her head - there was a phone in the choir room inside the church but the back door of the church was locked and her key for it was in her desk drawer. They would see her if she went to the front door. She couldn't go to the cottage since Miss Liz wasn't home. Maura McCarthy! She would run across the street and Maura would know what to do. She hiked up her long flowing summer caftan dress, kicked off her heels and started running across the courtyard.

Across the street, Danny McCarthy was sitting at the table on his screen porch getting ready to take his first bite of a tomato sandwich slathered in Duke's mayonnaise. Maura had just come outside with the tea pitcher. "Look Maura," he exclaimed. Maura looked up to see Reva running toward the street.

"Could be she got into a wasp nest or something," Maura said and ran to open the screen door. Just as Reva got to the curb, a police cruiser was coming down the street. Maura hurried down the driveway. She watched Reva wave her hands - the cruiser stopped and Jess Hamilton got out of the driver's seat. Reva had run so fast, she was out of breath. She tried to talk but all she could do was sputter.

"Slow down Reva - what's wrong?" Jess was the first to speak.

"Don't turn on your siren, Jess. Someone's in Rock's office and he has a gun."

"What on earth?" Maura started to ask more questions, but Jess interrupted.

"Reva, do you know who it is?"

"No sir - I've never seen the man in my life, but he's driving a motorcycle. It's on the other side of Rock's truck. He's a big one, alright - got lots of skin graffiti!"

Jess looked confused. "The motorcycle?"

Reva rolled her eyes. "No! The man. He's big and muscular and has all these funny looking tattoos all over his body. And worst of all, he's sitting right in front of Rock holding a shotgun. Just walk back there and see."

Jess got back in the cruiser and pulled it into Maura and Danny's driveway behind some shrubs to get it out of view. He didn't want the gunman to see it and do something rash. He'd heard Rock's voicemail and decided to drop by instead of waiting for him to come by his office. He motioned to Maura, "Take Reva and go into your house and lock your doors," he said. "I'm calling for backup." After making his call, he walked across the street and took his gun out of the holster. It's not your typical day in Park Place, he thought, and tried to stay out of sight until Officer Thompson could get there.

CHAPTER 27

*"*J*udge not, and you will not be judged; condemn not, and you will not be condemned; forgive, and you will be forgiven;*

~ Luke 6:37

And he gave some [to be] apostles; and some, prophets; and some, evangelists; and some, pastors and teachers; for the perfecting of the saints, unto the work of ministering, unto the building up of the body of Christ;

~ Ephesians 4: 11, 12

When Sonny Watson walked in the door, his presence in the room had been overwhelming. He was large and solidly built - more muscle than fat. He immediately put the gun case down on the sofa and turned around to shake Rock's hand. Rock shook it back but was speechless and Sonny laughed. "Reverend Clark, I apologize - I know I didn't make much of an impression on you at the livestock auction and I'm afraid I haven't made a good one today by bringing a gun in here. I didn't think how it would look until I saw your face when I walked in." All Rock could do was nod his head. Denying his reaction would be pointless - he had been afraid. He felt more at ease now, but why did he have a gun?

As if reading his mind, Sonny said, "I didn't want it to get stolen outside on my bike - it's sort of special to me.

I've been curious as to what you wanted to see me about. I called Grammy and Papa Jack last week and they told me you had been by to visit with them too. As a matter of fact, I'm going to their house when I leave here. I thought I would surprise them and spend the night - Papa loves to take Old Joe out coon huntin' and he's not able to navigate the woods by himself anymore. The season's not in, so we won't be shooting at any raccoons, but there's some mean snakes in those woods," he said pointing to the gun.

Rock had settled down enough to collect his wits. "Your grandparents were very welcoming when I visited – they even fed me." He was still shaken up and he hoped his voice sounded normal.

Sonny smiled. "They've been good to me - even when I didn't deserve it." He opened up the gun case and took out the gun. "This was Papa Jack's shotgun. I'm ashamed to say that back when I was getting into so much trouble, I pawned it time and time again. This time it's taken me months to track it down to buy it back." He held it in his lap like a prized possession.

Rock and Sonny had a good conversation. Rock told him about Holly and the words she had muttered. "'Sonny' - it makes sense that it would be a name - there's quite a few of us around. I don't know her - I've never been in that part of Ohio but it sounds like she could use our prayers," he said.

He told Rock about his earlier brush with the law and how he came to find salvation a few months back. "Of all things, it was in a bar," he said. "There was this guy in there handing out leaflets. My friends and I were giving him a hard time. I'll never forget what he said - he handed me his business card and looked me right square in the eye and said, 'Sonny, there's someone that loves you enough to never give up on you.'

I couldn't figure out how he knew my name, but come to find out it was a lucky guess. I thought he was talking about my parents and grandparents. I rebuked him. 'Who sent you'? I asked, "and who loves me enough to never give up on me?' He got right in my face - wasn't even intimidated by me."

Rock chuckled, "He's got one up on me then." Sonny laughed.

"And then the guy says, 'Sonny, it's God that loves you. He knows you by name and He wants you to know Him'. Now if that wasn't a message meant for me, I don't know what it was. I guess that fellow using my name personalized it for me. I got down on my knees right there in that bar. I asked him what I needed to do and he walked me through a prayer of repentence. I told God right out in front of all these baffled bikers that I wanted him to come into my heart and asked his forgiveness for my sins. I knew I didn't deserve it but I felt a peace right away that I was forgiven."

Rock was touched. What a ministry - going into bars with the likes of these big rough and tumble men - the kind that scare me half to death, he thought. He was curious about the man. "Who was it that witnessed to you, Sonny?"

"You know, that's the curious part. He left me some booklets and just disappeared. I called the number on the card later to thank him and it was a number for a church but no-one had ever heard of him. Whoever it was, he was an angel sent by the Lord himself; I'm convinced of that. I did join the church and they've helped me grow in my faith - the pastor has personally taken it upon himself to mentor me. It's a non-denominational church with people from every walk of life - just sinners like me trying to find our way. I think God wants to use me just like I am. I don't try to hide my tattoos and such because they get me in places where I can reach other lost people, if you know what I mean."

Rock did know what he meant. This new Christian was on fire - being fed by the Holy Spirit. And his new church was fueling the fire by filling his soul with the Word of God. Sonny's pastor, like Paul of the early Church, was urging his flock to use their spiritual gifts for the purpose of "building up the church." Rock felt ashamed of his own inadequacy in instilling that kind of evangelistic spirit in his church family. What had he been doing to feed his flock? Had his busyness kept him from keeping God's Word fresh and alive for his congregation? Churches were not immune to becoming stale and stagnant. He, himself had been called to be a pastor, "*for the perfecting of the saints, unto the work of ministering, unto the building up of the body of Christ.*" He had been trying to do his job but without the pizazz necessary to reach new Christians and non-believers.

This young man, newly convicted in Christ, made Rock think about how he stayed in his own little safe world, never venturing out of his comfort zone - content to care for people from a distance, but not wanting to become intimately entangled. He thought of Liz - why had he not nurtured their relationship? Sure, they were friends, but what was this feeling he had when she was near? Could it be love? That thought frightened him. He had loved before and that had not ended well. Could he ever work through those issues and love again? One thing was certain - it wouldn't just happen without some effort on his part.

Sonny's pastor apparently had the gift of evangelism. Rock had learned early in his ministry to accept the fruits of another person's spiritual gifts and he knew he could learn from him. When he mentioned it to Sonny, he gave him the phone number for his church. "He'll love talking to you," he said.

Out the corner of his eye, Rock saw Reva walk toward the back entrance of the building - then all of a sudden, she ran back towards the front. She must have left something in her car, he thought.

Sonny had picked up the jar of Mabel's jelly and was looking it over. "Homemade?"

"Yes," he said. "Mabel's finest. She makes the most mouthwatering jelly you've ever had the pleasure of eating. I have another jar at home, take that one and find out for yourself."

"Mabel? Hmm... she didn't look like a Mabel to me."

"You've met Mabel?"

"Well, I guess so," he said. "I came by here one day last week and you weren't here. This very attractive blonde with lots of flashy jewelry parked out at the road and walked up to me in the parking lot. She asked me if I minded putting a jar of jelly on your front porch. She said something about running late and it was your favorite, so I just bounded on up your front steps and left it there." He was alarmed at the expression that had come over Rock's face. "Maybe it was Mabel's daughter?"

Rock felt like someone had kicked him in the stomach. "Mabel doesn't have a daughter. Did you see what kind of car she was driving?"

"Boy, did I. The car was as flashy as her jewelry - a white Mercedes."

Rock slowly breathed in and out and tried to remain calm. "Could you identify her?"

Sonny looked confused. "Well, yes, I'm sure I could if I had to. I don't usually forget a pretty face," he said and smiled.

Rock heard a noise in the kitchen and figured Reva had come in. Just at that moment, the door from the kitchen area flew open.

"Freeze!"

Rock nearly jumped out of his skin and held his hands straight up in the air.

CHAPTER 28

It had taken some sorting out, but Rock finally convinced Jess Hamilton that he was not in any danger from the gentle giant seated on his sofa with a shotgun. Rock showed Jess the letter from the post office and told him of his suspicions that Mary Jo was involved. Reva brought in her peach cobbler and made a pot of coffee. Sonny had won her over by oohing and ahing over it, but Reva told him with her best sassy voice that the next time he came in the office, he'd better have a decent shirt on. "Why, I get seasick just trying to wade through all that ink," she said and pretended to cover her eyes.

"I do think you're right, Miss Reva," he said. "There's a time and place for everything." They had made their way outside and he walked over to his bike and got a neatly pressed shirt from his saddlebag and put it on over the sleeveless undershirt. "Grammy's not wild about all this ink either," he said, "and I need to be gettin' on down the road before they give up on me." As they stood outside, he and Rock shook hands and promised to stay in touch. Jess shook his hand too. "We may need you to identify that it was Miss Hilton that brought the jelly if it comes to that," he said. Sonny mounted his bike and pulled out a business card and gave it to Jess. It had his cell number and the front was imprinted with a drawing of a motorcycle and the words, *Ride Hard, Pray Harder.* "I'll be glad too. I'm not too fond of cat killers," and he revved up and rode away.

Maura walked back across the street to tell Danny what was going on and Eileen called Rock to tell him he could pick up Theo. "Happiest news I've had all day," he told Reva.

"You go on," she said. "I'll lock up."

***

With Theo in the cat carrier, Rock stopped by the Golden Palace and picked up a takeout order of Beef Lo Mein. As soon as he brought the carrier in the house, Theo started meowing. Rock opened it up and the cat made a mad dash for the laundry room looking for his food bowl. As Rock poured from the bag, Theo nudged his head in and once again had cat food raining down on his head. "You haven't changed a bit, old boy," he said. "You're still wolfing it down." Rock put the kettle on the stove and when the water had heated, he poured it into a cup and steeped a tea bag. He carried his laptop along with his takeout and tea on a tray to the study and looked over his email messages while eating. He was hoping to at least hear something from Liz. She sometimes took her laptop down the mountain to the coffee shop in Rocky Falls and used their WiFi. He checked his Inbox - nothing. He checked his Spam folder - still nothing. With a new resolve, he picked up the phone and called the number at the cabin - no answer. Maybe this was just not meant to be, he thought. Theo came bounding in the room and jumped up on his chest. He settled on his lap and started purring loudly. "Well at least I have you Theo," he said. And his resolve flew out the window.

Over the next few days, the puzzle pieces started falling together and everything happened so fast that Rock quickly returned to his old routine of staying busy. The veterinarian's toxicology report had come back early identifying the poison that Theo ingested as a pesticide. Jess Hamilton sent the unlabeled jelly to a lab to see if it contained the same pesticide after Rock told him about Mary Jo's previous background as a chemist and her purported invention of an environmentally friendly pesticide that had been lauded and published in scientific journals. The journal article had stated that its chemical composition could be easily changed by adding or taking away substances to make it either more environmentally safe or more toxic as pests developed a resistance to it. Jess explained to Rock, "There's nothing we can do until we get that report. If our suspicions are right, you could be in danger, Rock. "I'll get an extra patrol duty for the church and the manse."

"There's no need to do that Jess. I can't imagine her doing anything else. At least now I know how bitter she is. It's sad, isn't it?"

"Sad and dangerous Rock. Be careful."

CHAPTER 29

"*F*or *by grace you have been saved through faith; and that not of yourselves, it is the gift of God; not as a result of works, that no one should boast.*"

~ Ephesians 2: 8-9

Peter Braem called Rock on Saturday morning to tell him that Holly had been transferred back to Clancy Memorial and was healing well. He had started reducing her meds to slowly bring her out of the coma and had given Rebecca permission to bring Abby by to see her later in the day.

Rock also received a call from Wanda Burns. She had called to tell him she wouldn't be at the Stewardship meeting on Thursday night. She had gone down to the coast to try to finish her book.

"The grandchildren are in and out of my house every day since school let out," she said. "There's just too many distractions and I needed a change of scenery. I look out the window here and feel as if I'm in a little New England fishing village with the serene coves of water, shrimp boats pulled up to the dock, fishermen putting their boats out to sea and a much simpler way of life. And I thank the good Lord that I am right here - where I am - surrounded by His beauty. If I can't write surrounded by all this, I should put down my pen."

"Can we trade places?" he asked. "My office would be

a good change of scenery for you." She just laughed.

"I just wasn't getting any inspiration in Park Place," she said, "but the words have been flowing since I got here."

"Enjoy it Wanda. I'm just jealous."

It was a beautiful morning and Theo was on his lap. He was making his final preparations for Sunday's sermon titled *Fruits of the Spirit* with his Scripture readings from Galatians 5. As he read through the verses, he thought of Edie Mosher - especially verse 26. *'Let us not be desirous of vain glory, provoking one another, envying one another.'*

Edie was a wealthy woman but she seemed envious of what other people had; not the material things, but she seemed to resent their happiness. She had provoked many people in the congregation with her harsh, judgmental words - even causing some people to move their membership. His peacekeeping skills were always on high alert when Edie was around. His conscience bothered him again that he had not driven out to see her. "I'll go and get it over with," he said to Theo as he lifted him off his lap and then settled him back in the chair when he got up.

He drove up the long winding driveway that led to Edie's home. She and her husband, John had moved to Park Place ten years ago when John had taken an early retirement after a heart attack. He had been a Wall Street stockbroker. They had first moved to Charlotte where their son and his wife lived, but later bought the old Wallace place - a beautiful old home built in 1906. They joined Park Place Presbyterian shortly after. It had been two or three years ago that John had a second heart attack - this time a massive one that he didn't survive. Edie had not always been bitter, but when John died, her spirit died within her.

Rock knocked on the door. Edie's son, Paul opened the door and invited him in. "Mom's been real anxious to see you." Rock made no excuses.

"Paul, I'm sorry I haven't been by to see her."

"Don't apologize - I've sometimes wanted to put off visiting her myself," he said with a grin. "It hasn't been easy - but she's my mother." Rock followed him down the hallway. "She just had some things on her mind she wanted to say to you." He smiled and winked. "She's out on the sun porch with our daughter, Jessica, and her new baby."

Oh no, Rock thought, what does she want to say to me? I'm in for it now. But he didn't voice his thoughts and just smiled back. "So that makes her a great grandmother. Congratulations, I didn't know."

"Yes, and I can't wait for you see how the great-grandmother is doing and meet the latest addition to our family, Mary Grace. Mother named her."

When Edie Mosher saw Rock walk in, she took her cane from beside the chair. She pointed it at him and he cringed inside. Then she smiled. "I was afraid you wouldn't come - and I wouldn't have blamed you," she told him as he took a seat on the wicker settee. She waited until Rock settled in his seat.

"I hope you're doing well, Miss Edie. Paul told me about little Mary Grace." He looked over at the baby and she was all smiles. It's no wonder Reva loves babies so much, he thought. They are cute and cuddly. "She's a sweetheart."

Edie smiled. "She is a little angel, isn't she? But that's not what I wanted to see you about." Rock turned his attention back to Edie and braced himself for her words.

"I've wanted to tell you how your sermon on Pentecost Sunday affected me." She put her cane back down against her chair. "When you talked about the Holy Spirit and how it fills the heart of the new believer, something happened to my heart."

Rock had dreaded this visit and couldn't believe what he was hearing. He just sat there and let her continue. "The Holy Spirit just seemed to fill it up and it's been full ever since. Rev Rock, I considered myself a Christian - went to church every Sunday, said my prayers once a day and took a peek inside my Bible every now and again. New believer? I had always been a believer or so I thought."

Edie hung her head for a moment and then looked up at Rock. "I became a bitter old woman when my John died. I quit trying to do good deeds to get into heaven which is what I thought it took. I didn't think about all the good deeds the people of Park Place had done for me during my grief-stricken days; I was too busy being miserable so I made everyone around me suffer. I was floored when you hit me with the clincher of your sermon that Sunday with your reading from Ephesians."

Rock remembered the passage and said, "*For by grace you have been saved through faith; and that not of yourselves, it is the gift of God; not as a result of works, that no one should boast.*"

"That's it - grace, not works. I barely made it out of church that day. I was too emotional to go out the front door. Carleen Foster saw my tears and walked with me out the back door and to my car. It didn't seem to faze her that just a few months ago, I had spoken so sharply to her because her grandbaby was whimpering a little in church and I fussed that she should have taken him out so the rest of us could hear. But she didn't hold it against me. She just hugged me tight when she saw I was crying and offered to drive me home." She paused for a minute, but Rock waited, not wanting to break the spell.

"Since then, I've been going around to everyone that I've hurt and trying to make it right. Most of them have forgiven me but some haven't. I'll just keep trying."

Rock was speechless for a moment - this was not what he had been expecting when he came for a visit. "I think I owe you an apology next," she said. "I'm afraid I haven't been very nice to you and I'm sorry." He moved closer to her chair and took her wrinkled hand in his. She reached for a tissue. "I've been shedding quite a few tears lately," she said.

"It comes from a softening of the heart," he said and grabbed a tissue for himself.

She smiled at him and he marveled at the change in her appearance. Her eyes were no longer accusing and bitter, but were shining bright. "I have my family back," she said, pointing at the three generations sitting with her on the porch. "I drove them away, but they've forgiven me." Her expression changed and she looked thoughtful for a moment. "Forgiveness is a thing of beauty, isn't it?" He nodded and she continued.

"Now you take Liz for example, who lives in the old manse - I think she's a friend of yours?" Rock nodded. "She's a fine woman - the kind that would never grow old and bitter." She looked at him to see if he understood. "The kind you wouldn't want to see slip through your fingers." She paused for effect.

"You see, I hurt her worst of all when I derided her one day at the post office for laughing and being happy - it had not been long since she lost her husband. I told her she must not have loved him very much or she wouldn't be laughing so. I could see the pain in her eyes, but I didn't apologize at the time. I did feel guilty but I kept my silence."

Edie looked at him to see his reaction. He could tell she was ashamed of the things she had said. Liz had never said anything to him about this, but it was not her way to talk about anyone.

"When I worked up enough courage to apologize to her, I called her one Saturday morning and asked if she could come see me. She didn't hesitate - she came right over. She was so kind and accepted my apology immediately. I told her that in the places John and I had lived before moving here, my apologies would not have been so readily accepted and I asked her what was different here in Park Place - nearly everyone I had asked had forgiven me. Do you know what she said?"

Rock shook his head, but he knew that Liz would have been kind to her. It was just her nature.

"I guess I was expecting her to get all pious about her faith and give me some frivolous pat answer. When you've been bitter for as long as I have, you get suspicious of people's motives."

She straightened up in her chair and tried to pull her grey cashmere shawl around her shoulders. Paul got up out of his chair and helped her. She smiled at him. "Thank you, Paul."

She turned back to face Rock. "She's witty, that one! It was the best possible comeback she could have given."

Rock was curious. "What did she say?"

"She teased me and said that God fashioned Southerners after Himself and they have the same attitude about grace that He does - it's free for the asking. She said some people call it Southern Charm, but she thinks it's more than that. Southerners are gracious and kind, she said. They're naturally forgiving or most of them anyway. Southern Grace is what she called it. I told her that I wanted some of that Southern Grace. She said to just stick around long enough and hang out with the right people and it would sneak up on me."

Edie turned her head and looked at Rock. "I like that girl!"

"So do I." Rock laughed but he was touched. He was finding that he had just been seeing the surface of the heart of Liz. They had shared a common grief upon losing Ron; her grief of course, stronger than his. He had witnessed her faith and spirit and had been in awe of it. But now he was seeing her from a different perspective; through the eyes of someone else. She had been kind to Edie and made her feel at ease with her apology.

As he stood up to say goodbye, Edie reached out her hand. "That's a special young lady that lives in your backyard, Rev Rock. I've been given another chance for a relationship with the ones I love and care about. I know you're a busy man trying to handle all the goings on of the church, but please don't be so busy chasing butterflies that you forget she's there."

Chasing butterflies? Is that what he'd been doing? He had a visual of an elusive butterfly lighting on flower after flower, and him running along halfheartedly trying to keep up with it. Yes, that's exactly what he'd been doing.

***

Sunday's service was a joyous one. The choir's anthem was awesome. Jenny Wilson, the organist and choir director was not aware of her own talent. She kept telling Rock that she was doing an injustice to the new organ. "I'm not a trained organist," she would say. "You need to find someone who can utilize all its features." Her words fell on deaf ears because she was amazingly talented and everyone else knew it whether she did or not.

It had been a long time since Edie's whole family had come to church, but there they were seated on the front pew - her son, daughter-in-law and their two grown children. Even little Mary Grace was there, being passed around from one to the other.

Betty Ann Williams and her husband, Roy were there. Her grandchildren had come for a two-week summer vacation. She and Roy shook Rock's hand on their way out of church. "Come join the fun at our house," she asked sincerely. "I cooked enough for an army." How could he refuse?

He had never seen such a spread and ate with gusto.

He spent the entire afternoon playing a game of softball with the children and was worn out when he got back home. It was a good kind of tired though. He needed the exercise and the company. Betty Ann had packed him a leftover plate for supper but he was still too full from lunch to eat it. He fed Theo a few bites of the ham and then settled in with his Sunday paper. After drifting off to sleep a few times, he took his shower and went to bed.

CHAPTER 30

"Reverend Clark?"

"Yes."

"This is Patty Gamble at Clancy Memorial Hospital. I hope I didn't wake you." Not at all, he wanted to say - I get up with the birds every morning. But he didn't.

"It doesn't matter," he said, "It was time for me to wake up anyway."

"I've called Dr. Braem and he asked me to call you. The night nurse noticed that Miss Spencer seemed much more restless during the night. Dr. Braem thinks she may be coming out of the coma."

"Tell him I'll be there in twenty minutes."

Peter Braem was already in the room when Rock arrived. "How did you get here so fast?" Rock asked. He knew Pete lived on Country Club Drive over in Avonwood - at least ten miles out of town.

"They reached me on my cell phone. I was already en route to make my morning rounds so I could get back to my practice. They've overbooked me at the office - it's going to be a long day." Peter was examining Holly's eyes with a penlight. She stirred and made a moaning sound.

"Is she in pain?"

"I don't think so - moans and groans are common for someone coming out of a coma. There's a good bit of eye movement this morning. By mid-afternoon I expect she'll become at least somewhat aware of her surroundings." He put his penlight back in his pocket. "What are you doing here so early?"

"The nurse called me to tell me Holly may be coming out of the coma. She said you asked her to call."

"Yes, but I didn't tell her you needed to come right away. I just thought you would want to know. I guess I should have made myself clearer when I asked her to call you."

"That's okay - I did want to know. Should I go get Abby?"

"No, I want to evaluate Holly first to see how much she remembers. I'm expecting a full recovery, but in the beginning, she may have memory loss and confusion."

"Can she hear us now?"

"Possibly," said Peter. "I'm going to put her under full observation until I can get back this afternoon. If she wakes up, they'll call me."

"I can round up some women from the church to sit with her," Rock said.

Peter looked around the room. He had been impressed by the little touches of home here and there brought in by the women of the church. There were throw pillows on the chairs, a knitted shawl at the foot of the bed and even a small colorful quilt hanging on the wall opposite the bed. "That would be nice, Rock. It'll be good for her to wake up with someone who cares sitting in the chair beside her."

***

Rock stopped at the end of his driveway. The

newspaper had been thrown just a few feet from the curb and he noticed that Maura and Danny's was in about the same spot on the other side of the street. He threw his in the car and walked up their driveway. Danny was watering the flower garden near the garage. He threw up his hand and waved and Rock waved the paper. Maura walked out from the screen porch with a pitcher of lemonade. "I see you have our newspaper. That'll save me a few steps. Come on up and have a glass of lemonade - I was just going to call Danny in - it's hot out here today." Danny put the water hose away and started up the steps.

"It is a scorcher, isn't it? A good cold drink of lemonade sounds good right about now," Rock said as he followed Danny onto the porch.

He relayed the news about Holly to the two of them and asked Maura if she could round up someone to sit with Holly for the rest of the afternoon.

"I'll call Betty Ann. I would go myself, but we're trying to prepare for company. My baby boy is coming home from California this weekend to help us celebrate Danny's birthday."

"Well that's a treat," said Rock. "He doesn't get home often, does he?"

"Only at Christmas," Danny said. "His job keeps him busy - he works for a big tech company out there developing software for the aviation industry. It's a good paying job, but he works too hard."

Maura's face grew soft. "It's just because we're his parents that we worry about him. He doesn't seem to get much time off, but everyone thinks the same thing about their children. Sonny is just special to us because he was our only boy in a house full of girls."

It took a few seconds for it to register - Sonny! Rock tried to remain attentive and calm. He had forgotten that young Danny was called Sonny by just about everyone who knew him. How could he have forgotten – they had lived across the street from the church all their lives and Rock had known this kid since he was about ten years old. If it'd been a snake it would 'a bit me, he thought.

"Didn't Sonny go to school in Ohio?" he asked.

"Yes, he did," Maura answered. "Ohio State University – home of the Buckeyes. He won an academic scholarship, but he also played football. We had to quit rooting for the Gamecocks while he was there – it just didn't feel natural."

Rock didn't know what to say. Maura could sense from his odd expression that something was troubling him. "Is something wrong, Rock," she asked. He knew he would have to share his suspicions.

***

Maura paced back and forth on the porch. "I would like to say that it can't be so, but I know as well as you do that young men and women do not always act wisely when they think they're in love. I just don't understand it though. If Holly was pregnant and told Sonny, I just know he would do the right thing and not just abandon her." She looked pleadingly at Danny. "Wouldn't he?"

Danny nodded his head. "I think so Maura. That boy has a heart of gold. I just think it's a coincidence."

"But remember, Danny? He was so heartbroken after

he moved to California because his girlfriend had called things off. We were worried about him being out there alone and heartbroken. Maybe Holly broke it off with him. That must be the reason."

"I still can't see it, Maura. If she was expecting a baby, why would she break up with him? And besides, there's got to be dozens of Sonnys around here."

"It seems there would be," said Rock. But so far, I've found only one and I've ruled him out without a doubt. I know it's a long shot, but maybe we could ask your boy about it."

"I think Danny is in denial," said Maura. "It sounds crazy, but I've felt a connection to that little girl ever since I laid eyes on her. Her hair is the exact same color as our oldest daughter Nicole's was at that age and there are other similarities too. Rock, I've changed my mind. I will go over to the hospital this afternoon and I'd like to ask a favor of you."

"Anything," said Rock.

"Could you go by and get Abby and bring her over too. I don't know why - but humor me, will you?"

Rock thought about Pete's words this morning, but this was a different situation. He knew he wouldn't mind. "I'll do it - what time?"

"I'll put some lipstick on and go over there now."

"Abby and I won't be far behind. I'll call Rebecca and tell her to have her ready." Rock rushed back down the driveway and got in the car. Was it a coincidence? His heart felt empty without Liz to share this with. "Liz, Liz, whatever am I going to do with you?" He shook his head and sighed. He looked in his rearview mirror and backed out on the street. "Or more realistically, what am I going to do without you?"

CHAPTER 31

Abby was excited as they drove toward the hospital. "Is my mommy awake yet?"

"No, not yet, Abby," Rock said. Abby looked disappointed. She had Bernie, freshly laundered and fluffed, in a small flowered backpack beside her and she pulled him out.

"Bernie and I will sing to her. That's how we usually wake her up on Saturday mornings at home when she's sleeping late." Rock felt good once again that they had helped make the decision to aggressively treat Holly's cancer. Abby adored her mother.

When they walked in the room, Maura was sitting beside the bed holding Holly's hand in hers. Abby ran to her and got up in her lap. "How's my mommy?"

Maura looked at the little girl with new eyes. This could be my grandchild, she thought. She lifted her up a little higher and sat her on the bed. "I've got Bernie here to cheer her up," she said, pulling the dog out of the bag again.

"He's a fine dog," Maura said. She held him up to her nose. "Hmmm - he doesn't smell like a dog at all!"

"That's because Miss Rebecca washed him and put some baby powders on him," she said, holding him up to her own nose.

"That's what he smells like! I knew I recognized that scent."

Holly stirred in the bed and moaned softly. "Hi

Mommy!" Abby moved closer and held the dog out to her mother. "Bernie and I came to see you and make you feel better." Holly stirred again. Abby looked up at Rock. "I think she knows we're here."

"I'm sure she does," said Rock. *Or at least I hope she does*, he thought.

Abby got very close to her mother's face. "This is our magical song," she told Maura. "I'm going to sing it to her and see if she wakes up. It always puts me to sleep, but since it's magic, maybe it'll wake her up."

"Who told you it was magic," said Maura.

"Mommy did. She said it was my daddy's song. He had to go away before I ever knew him, you know." This was the first time Rock had heard her speak of her dad. Rebecca had told him that she had never mentioned him. She looked at Maura with a solemn little face. "But he must have been magical too if this was his song." She started singing a pleasant melody in a sweet, soft voice. "Don't worry if you can't understand it the first time. I'll sing it again so you can."

Du, du liegst mir im Herzen
du, du liegst mir im Sinn.
Du, du machst mir viel Schmerzen,
weißt nicht wie gut ich dir bin.
Ja, ja, ja, ja, weißt nicht wie gut ich dir bin.

Maura gasped. Rock looked over at her and saw her shocked expression. She was gripping the chair she was sitting in with both hands. He walked over and took her hand and then led her to the door. "Maura, what's wrong!"

"I need to walk out for a minute." He looked back at Abby - she was still singing and holding Bernie up to Holly's face. He knew she would be fine while they stepped out of the room. When they got outside the doorway, Maura steadied herself by holding on to Rock's arm. There were tears in her eyes.

"I have a music box at home on my mantel that plays that same song. My brother Jim gave it to me when he came home from Germany and I sang that lullaby to my children every night as I tucked them in bed. He was my older brother - twenty years older in fact - and he committed suicide on my fourth birthday." She stood there for a minute. "It's such an uncommon song, Rock. This is much more than a coincidence." She turned loose of Rock's arm. "I need to call Danny."

Rock led her into the family waiting room and handed her the phone. When she finished her conversation, she walked back into the hallway where he was waiting. "He's going to call Sonny right now," she said. "Let's go back in the room. I want to be with my granddaughter."

CHAPTER 32

It had been an emotional day. Danny had not been able to reach Sonny. His office said that he was in an all-day conference in Seattle. But there was no doubt in any of their minds that Abby's father was Sonny McCarthy. After Rock took Abby back to the children's home, he came back to the hospital. Peter Braem was there assessing Holly's progress. "It's still going to be awhile before she's fully awake." He spoke to Maura, "you can go on home now. I have an off-duty nurse lined up to stay in the room overnight. We'll know more in the morning."

Rock walked Maura to her car. "What a day," she said. "This morning I thought I had four grandchildren and now I find out I may have five. I'm having a hard time taking it all in."

He checked by the church office to see if he had any messages but Reva was already gone. While he was going through the mail she had picked up at the post office, he had a phone call from Jess Hamilton on his cell phone.

"Bingo," he said. "Thanks to the cooperation of Diamond Chemicals, we've been able to identify the toxin found in your cat's blood sample and it matches the very type of pesticide Mary Jo Hilton helped develop. There are some slight alterations, but it was similar enough that Judge Parker issued a search warrant for us to search her house and office."

Instead of feeling Jess' excitement, Rock felt rather

sick to know he had dated someone who was capable of poisoning someone. By the grace of God, he had not eaten the jelly, but he knew, and Jess knew that it was meant for him.

"If she had set out to poison your cat, we would just be charging her with animal endangerment or animal cruelty, but poison placed in food that's meant for human consumption is a different matter. If our search is productive, she could be charged with attempted murder."

Rock hung up the phone and walked outside. He looked at the empty house beyond the path and didn't like what he saw so he walked back inside his own empty house, made himself a cup of coffee and settled into his chair. He had gone from being surprised when Liz had not come home right away to being concerned that something was wrong. Now he just felt mad - mad at himself for not making more of an effort to get through to her and puzzled and mad with her for being gone for so long without calling to let him know she would be staying longer than planned. And angrier still that she was not answering her phone. Peggy! Why didn't he think of her before now? He would call Peggy.

He was beginning to think the whole mountain village had disappeared when Peggy's phone rang and rang with no answer. He was about to hang up when a breathless Peggy answered.

"Rock, yes, I caught your voice. How are you doing? What? I think we have a bad connection. I'm catching about every other word you're saying......What's that again? Liz? Is that what you said Rock? No, she's not here. She drove down to Atlanta on Saturday. Ron's father passed away and the funeral was today. What's that? Surgery - are you having surgery? When? I hope you'll be okay.... Not you? Oh that's good..... Polly? Cancer?..... Who's Polly? Liz will know who it is I guess."

Rock was getting frustrated. He could hear Peggy perfectly fine - why couldn't she hear him? He tried again.

"I can't hear a word you're saying Rock. We had a storm last week and it played havoc with all our phones. What? I still can't understand you. Call her back tomorrow. She should be home...."

Home? 'Here' home or 'there' home, he wondered. Blast it!

Her cell phone; if she's in Atlanta, she'll have service, he thought. He scrolled down to her number and pushed the Call button. It rang once and went to voicemail. He sighed. Her voicemail must be full. During the time she had been on the mountain there would have been phone calls and messages left. She had probably forgot to check it when she got back into a service zone. Drat!

He turned on his laptop and checked his email - nothing. Theo had jumped up on the back of his armchair and was trying to settle down for a nap. "She sure doesn't care anything about me Theo." He pulled the cat down from the back of the chair, sat him on his lap and held his paws up in the air. "I'll pour you a drink and we'll have a pity party." Theo was loving the attention. He moved Theo's front legs back and forth in a swaying motion and sang to the tune of the Bobby Bare song his roommate sang in college when he came home after a night of partying. He hadn't heard the song in years.

"*Pour me another Tequila, Sheila.*" Theo jumped for dear life down from his lap and ran and hid. "Ah, come on Theo, don't be a spoilsport." He took another sip of his coffee and thought that maybe his frustration was driving him insane. "How many preachers dance with cats and sing bar songs?" he wondered aloud.

A few feet away in his bedroom, the house phone was facing toward the wall where at some point Theo had managed to move it. While walking across it and stepping on the buttons, he had also managed to turn the volume down. The screen was dim - there was no sound but it was flashing, *3 new messages.*

CHAPTER 33

L iz was nearing Spartanburg on Interstate 85 where she would need to either take the Asheville exit to go to Rocky Falls or the Columbia exit to go toward home to Park Place. She had left in a hurry for Atlanta so her laptop and some of her clothes were still at the cabin. She was in a sad state of mind. She had loved her father-in-law. Ron had been so much like him. Her mother-in-law had been grateful that she had come for the funeral and asked her to stay for a couple of days to help her get things sorted out. Liz had stayed one more night, but felt she needed to leave the sorting out to Carolyn's other children - Ron's brothers and sisters. It had been great to see them all. Ron's mother had lost a son and now her husband, but her other children lived close by and would take care of her. It was time for her to pull away.

When she reached the I-26 exit toward Asheville, she took it. She still hadn't heard a word from Rock and her heart felt empty. She had felt so at peace at the cabin. She would go back and stay at least another night or two - maybe longer. It had been almost two weeks since she left Park Place and the messages she had recently left on his answering machine had been ignored. After the last one telling him about her trip to Atlanta, she had given up on hearing from him. She was hurt and surprised. She had been so sure that he was feeling a little of the same spark that she felt. Well, spark was an understatement on her part. She now realized that she loved him. Their easy bantering of late had been more flirtatious than mere talking. But even if he hadn't felt the spark, their friendship should have meant something to him. He had been so attentive to her for the past two years - maybe he was trying to step back and away from the relationship. Had she been a burden to him? She wondered if their moments together had been out of a sense of duty to his best friend. Well, if that's what he wanted, she would give him his space. When she got back to the cabin she would call Reva and check up on Holly Spencer and little Abby. She would ask Reva to go check on the house and water her flowers. She had shown her once before where she hid the spare key. She had no obligations until mid-August when the new school year would begin. It would be lonely on the mountain without Peggy to keep her company - they may be crossing paths right about now with Peggy on her way to Florida to visit family. She thought about her land line at the cabin. If it was still out of order, she would be out of luck calling Reva since there was no cell service on the mountain. I'll call her now, she decided and exited off the Interstate. She pulled into a Wendy's parking lot and got out her phone. She had not used it in Atlanta and was surprised to find her voice mailbox was full. With renewed hope, she checked them all and cried softly when she saw there was not a single one from the man she had fallen hopelessly in love with. She looked at her watch. Reva would be in the office so she dialed the number hoping Rock would not answer. On the third ring, Reva answered. "Liz honey, where are you?" The genuine caring in Reva's voice dug deep into the emotions Liz had been trying to hide. She started sobbing.

CHAPTER 34

Jess had asked Rock to stop by the station after the Police Department's successful search of Mary Jo's house and office. "We found it at her office," he said. "It's a small vial with a red warning sticker on it. There's no odor so the cat wouldn't be repelled by it. If we had found nothing more, we would have had to wait until it was tested to arrest her, but the clincher was sitting on the same shelf behind her desk - a new box of half-pint canning jars with one jar missing. And to top it off we found a half empty pint jar of store brand blackberry jelly in her refrigerator. Still, that would have just been circumstantial evidence without her confession."

"Confession?" Rock couldn't believe it.

"Yeah, I was surprised too. I've always heard this girl was a genius and she must be pretty smart with chemicals and such, but she sure doesn't have any common sense. You won't believe what she had the nerve to say."

"I'm afraid to ask?"

"When I picked up the vial and asked her what was in it, she said - in a very whiny voice I might add - that it was just a small amount - only enough to make you sick."

Rock looked incredulous. "But she almost killed my cat!"

"Do you want to see her? She's called her parents but they haven't come by to post bail yet to get her out."

"Heavens no! I might be tempted to strangle her and you would have to lock me up too."

***

Jamie Webster caught Rock before he walked into Holly's room. "She's awake." Before he could ask, she continued. "Dr. Braem is with her but should be out in just a minute." He waited at the door until Pete came out and led him to his office.

"She's been awake for about an hour, but she doesn't remember anything. It's not unusual - it could take days for her to get her memory back. She did speak - she asked for a cup of water."

Rock was relieved. "That's good, isn't it?" Pete nodded.

"I asked if she knew her name - she seemed to be struggling to remember it but she didn't respond. I told her Abby had been by to see her. There was no recognition at the mention of Abby's name."

"Oh no!" Rock sat down hard on the chair in front of Pete's desk, but Pete assured him that her memory would improve.

"There's a new twist to the story, Pete." Rock told him about the latest developments.

Maura had called him early to tell him they had finally reached Sonny before they went to bed. "Holly was his girlfriend in Columbus, Rock. He had no idea she was pregnant when he left. He's coming home but it's going to be somewhat of a different visit than we had planned. It's so complicated." Rock had agreed. I'll fill you in later," she had said.

Pete listened and nodded. "It is complicated. I don't

think we should spring all this on Holly right away. It would be too much for her."

"We can't spring it on Abby either. If it's true that Sonny is her father, she'll need to hear it from Holly when and if she's ready to tell her."

"Rock, is there anything I can do to help?"

"Yes - pray."

Rock drove back to the office in slow motion trying to absorb the happenings of the day. Holly's condition was unsettling, but his mind was still on his conversation with Jess at the police station. For the last two days, he had been frustrated and angry - there was no other way to put it. Instead of pulling into the office parking lot, he pulled up next to the back door of the church and got out. Just stepping into the empty sanctuary of this old church had always soothed his soul. It was God's house and He resided in every nook and cranny of the building, but more importantly in the hearts of the people who worshiped here.

The founding fathers had built the church to last with simple but aesthetically pleasing features. The magnificent arched windows were made up of fitted individual panes of opaque, pale green swirled stained glass. The dark mahogany wood archway behind the pulpit was made of beams from a local plantation and handcrafted by William Oliver, a descendent of one of the original members of the church. An early Eastlake settee and matching pair of chairs made up the seating area for the clergy. The tin-plated ceiling reached high up into the air but not quite high enough to hide that it was in need of restoration. The paint was beginning to flake off, but to Rock, it was part of the charm of the old church interior.

He sat for a moment on the front pew, then knelt at the altar. He knew that going forth with an angry heart was an obstacle hindering his relationship with God. He prayed that God would open his heart so that he could accept the spiritual guidance only He could give him. He prayed for Mary Jo and that she would be moved by God's grace. He prayed for Holly and Abby and the McCarthy family as they found their way through these new developments. And finally, he prayed for Liz that she would find happiness and peace. "And while I have your attention Lord, if it is Your will, let her happiness and peace include me."

He was surprised at his own prayer - it just came out of his mouth and he immediately was filled with doubt and wondered if he should take it back. He could imagine God with a sense of humor wagging his finger at him saying, "Too late now, Rocko - I'm already on it."

It had not been his intention to get out of his comfort zone and fall in love, but somewhere along the line, that's just what he had done. The realization that he loved her thrilled him and frightened him at the same time. He started whistling as he walked out of the church building and through the courtyard. The air was crisp and clear and the world seemed a brighter place again to the preacher whose tune was a little off-key walking down the path to his office. It's amazing what a few moments with God can do.

***

"What's got into you Reva?" he asked. "Have I done something?"

"Hmph! It's what you haven't done that matters."

The way she jerked her chair around and turned her back on him convinced him to keep his mouth shut. He thought of something he had grown up hearing his mother say all the time, 'if looks could kill' - well, if they could, Reva would be charged with murder if he didn't get out of here. And his own murder to boot, so he wouldn't be around to visit her in jail. What a tragedy - two women he knew in Park Place in jail – and a dead preacher. What one didn't accomplish, the other one did. He took his laptop and got out while the getting was good.

CHAPTER 35

He says, "Be still, and know that I am God;
I will be exalted among the nations,
I will be exalted in the earth."

~ Psalm 46:10 NIV

The rainstorm during the early morning hours had awakened him with claps of thunder and lightning flashes in the sky. It passed quickly though and Rock woke up to the sun filtering through his window and the sound of Irma Rembert's dog barking. His first thoughts were of Liz and his light-hearted promise to shoot some WD-40 at the dog to stop it from barking. The morning became even more pleasant when he heard the distinct sound of the paper smacking one of the columns on the porch. He loved it when he could just walk out on the porch with his slippers and robe on. Most mornings he had to get fully dressed to pick the paper up out of the ditch. As he finished up his morning prayers, he smelled the aroma of the coffee as it brewed when the automated timer turned it on. "Thank You Lord for a new start to a new day." When he stepped out on the porch, he saw Danny and Maura pull in their driveway and up to the front door. Sonny had taken an overnight flight and they had already picked him up from the airport. He saw Danny drop him off at the front door to unload his suitcases and then drive on into the garage.

He took his coffee and his Bible to his armchair. He felt a sense of relief that this was no longer his concern and he felt strangely liberated. He would let the McCarthy's work things out and when they needed him, they would call him. As Holly recovered, his responsibilities as her guardian would be over. There was a time to bow out and he felt that God was leading him to do so. He would stop his busyness and be still for a while. "*Be still and know that I am God.*" He distinctly heard God's voice and turned the pages to read more of the Psalms. As he thumbed through, he came upon Psalms 65 and saw some verses he had highlighted at some time or another - maybe for a sermon - he couldn't remember.

> *By awesome deeds you answer us with deliverance,*
> *O God of our salvation;*
> *you are the hope of all the ends of the earth*
> *and of the farthest seas.*
> *By your strength you established the mountains;*
> *you are girded with might.*
> *You silence the roaring of the seas,*
> *the roaring of their waves,*
> *the tumult of the peoples.*
> *Those who live at earth's farthest bounds are awed by your*
> *   signs;*
> *you make the gateways of the morning and the evening*
> *   shout for joy.*

The word 'mountains' had got to him. He knew without a doubt that God had led him to this scripture. He just had to be still to hear it.

***

Rock's family tree had a preacher in just about every branch. His grandfather had joked that if you shook it hard enough, you could get a bushel full of just about every denomination. He had known from an early age that he would preach and he'd been influenced in his calling by two of his uncles.

"You have the gift and the right spirit," his uncle Mike had told him - the same uncle that was now protesting at the other end of the line.

"Rock, this isn't the best of times. Jo Ann has gone with Eric to a seminar in Wilmington and left her three kids with me and Gladys. Gladys is about to lose her mind. She couldn't possibly handle the children at your church by herself with me in the pulpit."

Rock was desperate. "I'll get someone to help her with the kids. They'll only be in the sanctuary for fifteen minutes tops, then they go to nursery right after the children's sermon."

Jo Ann lived in Charlotte and was Mike and Gladys' only child. After Mike's retirement from a large church in Durham, they had moved to Sun's Up to be near her and had joined her church. On Rock's rare absences from the pulpit, Mike would fill in for him except when the entire Clark clan took their annual beach trip. Then Jim Jackson, the retired Baptist pastor in the community would fill the pulpit.

"I don't know Rock. The children are well-behaved at our church but this may get them off kilter."

"For heaven's sake, Uncle Mike, the kids will be fine. This is an emergency!"

"Well, why didn't you say so? Is something wrong with your parents?"

"No, that's not it. I would have told you that already." He decided to confide in Mike. "It's me, Mike. I think I've let someone special slip through my fingers."

"Pack your bags then and get the heck out of there! Those someone specials don't come around very often as you know first-hand. We'll be there with our pack of little hellions – prepare your church for the slaughter. On second thought, don't. You may have zero attendance."

By the time he got his overnight bag packed and was on his way out of town, the electronic sign at the bank was flashing 10:15 a.m. and seventy-eight degrees. He practiced what he was going to say to Liz for fifty miles down the interstate, the scenario playing out in his mind of how she would run into his arms and say, *Yes, Rock, I've been waiting for you to come to me. Yes, Yes, I love you.* But when he hit the last leg of the trip in Spartanburg, the fantasy played out and he was convinced that he was going to be humiliated. She would look at him coolly and say, *Rock, you poor dear man. I had no idea you felt that way about me. I thought we were just friends,* and he would have to go home a beaten man.

"Lord, help me find the words to say," he said. "I

know you didn't lead me up here just to find out she doesn't have the same feelings for me." His prayer bolstered his confidence as he drove up the mountain.

He pulled into her driveway and was relieved to see her car was there. He got out of the truck and started up the sidewalk. It's now or never, he thought. As he rounded the corner, he saw Earl sitting in one of the tall porch rockers whittling away at one of his wood carvings. He stood up when he saw Rock walk up the steps of the porch. Rock motioned with his fingers to his lips. "Where's Liz?" he whispered.

Earl understood and whispered back. "Miss Lisbeth is making coffee for her and hot chocolate for me. She's been watching for you for many days. I'll go home now." Rock nodded, shook his hand and whispered a silent thank you.

Earl turned around and started walking away. On second, Rock called back to him. "Wait a minute, Earl. Can I borrow your baseball cap?" Earl smiled and handed it over. He put on the cap and moved Earl's rocker so that it was facing the trout stream and only the back of the rocker was visible from the door. He started whistling just as Earl had been doing. He heard the screen door bang behind him and glancing sideways in her direction, watched as she started walking across the porch. There had been a recent rain shower and the cooler temperatures had greeted him as he drove up the long, winding road to the cabin. Liz was wearing a flannel shirt over a school-spirit t-shirt and a pair of faded jeans. His heart did flip-flops as he sensed her coming closer. She walked over and put the hot chocolate on the porch rail, and said, "Here's your cup, Earl. It's pretty hot so be very, very careful." It couldn't have worked out any better. She hadn't even looked at him.

As she turned to walk back to the porch swing, he spoke in a normal voice and said, "Thank you, Miss Lisbeth, but I'm so tired of being very, very careful."

He watched what seemed to be in slow motion as her coffee cup slipped out of her hand and fell to the floor. In one fluid movement, he got up from the chair, moving swiftly to swoop her out of the way so she wouldn't get burned.

"You do know how to make a grand entrance, Reverend Clark," she said, not bothering to move out of his embrace.

He reached down and brushed away the strands of hair that had fallen across her face and brushed his lips against her ear and whispered, "I've missed you, Liz Logan, and...." He paused for a moment but decided to just do it and not drag it out. "And I love you."

Caught off guard, she pulled back and looked at him, total surprise in her eyes. "I must be losing my hearing, Rock. Please repeat that." He smiled at her and started to say it over again, but she put her finger up to his lips. "Never mind, it wouldn't come out that perfect again." They stood there holding each other tight as if turning loose would break the spell. When they finally pulled apart, it was only briefly so that he could bend down and kiss the soft lips that seemed to be made only for his. She sighed and he felt his heart melt completely.

"Let's go home."

"I thought you'd never ask."

CHAPTER 36

I t's Saturday morning and the two rockers sitting side
by side on the cottage's porch are wet with the early
morning dew and a few brown and yellow leaves have
drifted onto the floor. An empty pitcher stands on the
little wicker table between the rockers. A line of ants
march like soldiers up the side of the pitcher and a lone
honey bee gleans the last of the sweet nectar at the
bottom of one of the two glasses sitting on the porch rail.
A pair of size 8 fuzzy pink bedroom slippers are in front
of the chair on the right and some size 11 men's plaid
slippers are in front of the chair on the left.

***

Down the path and across the street a young girl's
squeals of laughter can be heard over Irma Rembert's
barking dog. A pretty young woman with pale skin and a
pixie-cut of auburn hair sits on a screen porch beside a
petite older woman with graying hair and they laugh
together at the sounds of the child playing with a new
puppy. The younger woman sips on a small glass of
orange juice.

"Sonny says he can be home for Thanksgiving," she
says to her new mother-in-law. For the umpteenth time in
the past month, she looks at her pensively and asks, "do
you think he feels sorry for me Maura, or does he really
love me?"

Maura smiles at her. She has grown to love this young woman like her own daughter. She has been patient with her as her body and mind has healed from all she's been through.

"He loves you, my dear. I wish you could have seen his face when he walked into that hospital room for the first time. It was pure adoration. When he first moved to California, he was devastated when your father answered his phone calls and told him you had made up your mind and didn't want to see him again. He was so distraught, we were worried about him being all alone out there with no family or friends for support."

"My father was afraid he would lose me. He had just lost my mother and he had it in his mind that I would move away. It was the beginning of his dementia – I wouldn't have abandoned him but he didn't know that. As sad as I am that Daddy passed away last month, just knowing that he's in heaven with Mom makes me happy."

"Sonny has taken his vows seriously Holly. In sickness and in health - he will love and care for you and Abby. I'm just glad his employers are going to allow him to carry on his job from here." Holly smiles. Maura knows that she just needs reassurance now and then.

"Honey, where are you?" Maura jumps up when she hears Danny calling.

"I'll see what he needs and be right back."

Danny is in the kitchen when she walks back inside. "How's Holly this morning?"

"She's fine - she seems to be getting stronger every day, but she still needs reassurance now and then."

Danny pours himself a cup of coffee. "Have you heard from the newlyweds?"

"No, but I think they went off to the Bahamas or somewhere like that." She shakes her head. "Madge and Cap together - I never would have believed it if I hadn't gone to the wedding and seen it for myself."

"I'm not talking about Madge and Cap. Isn't it funny that we've had three weddings in Park Place in less than three months?"

"Oh, Rock and Liz," she answers. "I don't consider them newlyweds since they've been married about six weeks now. It is odd that we've had all these weddings in our church when it's been over a year since we had one at all. Rock and Liz, our Sonny and Holly, and now Cap and Marge, all married in such short order."

***

Back on the other side of the street again, a large house with a summer wreath on the door stands empty; a new manse with no one living in it.

A lone car with a *Be Happy* license plate is parked in front of an old carriage house converted into an office just a few steps away. One hundred and fifty-two newsletters are stacked on the desk of the lady with the warm chocolate complexion.

"Blast it!" she mutters as she starts putting on the stamps. "Do I have to do everything myself?" No one answers.

***

Two blocks away at the tiny post office, a heated exchange is going on between two friends. "I thought I was going to be in your dad-blasted book, but no-o-o, you had to up and write about two lost lovers in a New England fishing village. And after I told all my friends that I was your main character. I don't know what to think about you, Wanda Burns!"

"Don't blame me Betty. This place is just so boring; nothing ever happens around here. If something exciting ever happens, I'll write my next book and you'll be in it, I promise."

"Exciting! If you would'a got your nose out of that dog-goned notebook that you spend your time writing in, you would have seen 'exciting'. I just don't know about you, girl."

***

Back down the street and up the pathway to the porch with the rockers, white sheer curtains billow softly as the aroma of freshly brewed coffee from an automatically programmed coffee pot wafts out through those same windows. Inside the door, a pale pink sweater and a man's tan jacket hang from the hooks of a large antique oak hall tree. Lesson plans spill from a file folder on the bench beneath. A leather armchair sits in front of the fireplace. A worn Bible sits on the table beside the chair with the beginnings of a sermon highlighted in yellow in a nearby notebook.

Down the hallway and to the left is the door to a

bedroom where a still newlywed couple lay propped up on pillows drinking coffee. The man is speaking.

"I love this old house. I always have and I always will. Do you think the Session will approve of us living here?"

The woman speaks with a twinkle in her eye. "Things change, Rock. But I think they will - at least for a few months."

He looks dismayed. "A few months! Why only a few months?"

"Well, you know they did have a reason behind building a bigger house. They had a vision - and a correct one I might add - that someday their pastor would marry and start a family."

The look of joy on her face gives her secret away. She laughs as he looks at her with eyes the size of saucers.

"I did a home pregnancy test this morning when I went to the bathroom. When I came back from the kitchen with our coffee, I checked it."

"And...?"

"It must have happened on our honeymoon, and..."

The man doesn't let her finish. His kiss is enough to make Theo blush and the big cat who was once a scraggly kitten flies into the kitchen, jumps upon the windowsill with the checkered curtains and watches the red and yellow leaves fall from the trees one by one. A yellow butterfly flits back and forth around the spent flowers that need to be cut back. There's no one there to chase it.

The End

AUTHOR'S BIO

Glenda Manus lives in Van Wyck, South Carolina with her husband, Henry, and their cat, Theo. It's a small Southern community much like the fictional town of Park Place in this, her first novel. "It's a little slice of Heaven," she says. "Everyone should have the opportunity to experience small-town Southern life – if not through a real visit, then a virtual visit through the eyes and words of an author who's lived there."

Made in United States
Orlando, FL
01 September 2022